# Kwamboka's

# Inquiry

## Arthur Dobrin

Nsemia

First Edition: March 2017
Published by Nsemia Inc. Publishers (www.nsemia.com)


Edited By: Verah Omwocha
Cover Concept & Illustration: Arthur Dobrin
Cover Design: Linda Kiboma
Layout: Bethsheba Nyabuto

Note for Librarians:
A cataloguing record for this book is available from Kenya National Library Services.

ISBN: 978-1-926906-52-2

# Dedication

This book is dedicated to two wonderful families, the Ong'esas and the Marangas, with love and admiration.

# About the Author

**Arthur Dobrin** is an American author, Professor Emeritus of Management, Entrepreneurship and General Business at Hofstra University and Leader Emeritus of the Ethical Humanist Society of Long Island.

Dr. Arthur Dobrin served two years in the Peace Corps with his wife, Lyn, in Kenya. He has maintained his interest in Kenya since, having returned with his family and having led educational safaris to Kenya for Adelphi University School of Social Work. He has published two novels, a collection of short stories and a book of poems all set in Kenya. He and Lyn directed the Kenya Project, a program that provides funding for an elementary school in Kisii.

Arthur Dobrin has also been a visiting scholar at Nanjing Normal University, Nanjing, China; Makerere University, Kampala, Uganda; Kisii College, Kisii, Kenya; the Gusii Technical College, Kisii, Kenya; and an exchange professor at Claflin University, in South Carolina, an historical black college.

## COVER PICTURE

Peace N. Hudgens used here with permission.

# TABLE OF CONTENTS

# Kwamboka

### 28 Feb. 2009
### 9 A.M.

IT IS MORNING IN KABUNGU. The ground still shimmers with dew, as the sun has just breached the crowns of the tulip trees that line the east side of the church compound. While the air is cool, the nails of the few wooden chairs exposed to the sun are hot to the touch. By mid-day hundreds of people from the district will fill the broad lawn and by the day's end there will be no more room for guests to add their names to the books put out for their signatures and messages of condolence. But now there are only a few workmen setting down a wooden table taken from the church's social hall. Behind the table, from which speakers will present their eulogies, is the new brick church with its tripled-arched portico and blue metal roof, and beyond that a sea of waist-high tea bushes rising to the hill's crest.

A few mourners join Lucy Kombo. She is waiting in the white tent set aside for dignitaries who will be arriving throughout the day to take their turn to speak. Several women with *kangas* wrapped as skirts are seated on the grass, their children playing quietly beside them; women more formally dressed are in rented chairs. Men are milling around—church elders mainly, wearing jackets and ties. They will help supervise the day's events. Lucy, the president of the board of the Malaika School for Little Angels, is there with Pastor Kennedy Okemwa— the minister scheduled to give the opening prayer. As master of ceremonies, he will introduce the speakers who will eulogize Sarah Kwamboka, the school's founder.

Although Kwamboka didn't belong to the African Independent Church of Christian Disciples, she would have approved of Lucy's choice in selecting Pastor Okemwa for his role in her funeral service. The minister is an ardent supporter of the Malaika School and many of the children of his congregants have been pupils there. It was evident to Lucy, who knew her better than anyone in Kabungu, that Kwamboka liked the pastor more than any other Christian minister in the district.

Kwamboka often enjoyed being with Okemwa, a thin man with a receding hairline, a man ten years her junior. He had kind eyes and a comforting voice, and the patches of gray in his goatee were attractive. He, like her, had studied abroad, though his studies were at a small evangelical college in Iowa, far from her secular education in Nairobi and London. In the last several years, she would admit to herself that she had grown fond of the minister. Her preference, though, was for nights by herself, enjoying the solitude of looking into the vastness of the night sky. Yet she was glad for his company, infrequent as it was, and the intellectual stimulation he could provide. Despite this, the visits to one another's home became even less frequent in the last year as she became happier in her cloistering, working on her collection of stories, and he busier with trying to keep his congregation together in the face of growing competition from Pentecostal churches.

\*\*\*\*

## 2005

"Do you believe in God, professor?" Pastor Okemwa asked one day as he sipped a cup of tea with Kwamboka in the school office. Kwamboka shifted her heavy body on the slatted wooden chair.

"Yes," she answered. "How can you not when you hear the chorus of birds every morning? There's a wonder in it."

The pastor nodded in understanding.

"And heaven, professor?" Okemwa slurped the sweet milky tea in a room heavy with the smell of damp concrete. He didn't raise his eyes from the cup's metal lip.

"Just listen," she said, turning her head to the opening of the school's playing field. It was mid-morning break and the youngest pupils were clapping and singing as they paraded with their teacher in circles on the grass. "Children's laughter is the sound of heaven."

"Agreed," he said. "And what about our final rewards? Do you believe in that, too?"

It had been a long time since Kwamboka had been asked about her theological beliefs. More typically, except at election time when politics was on everyone's mind, her talk, even with Okemwa, was more prosaic—the rains, drought, inflation and the price of food, illness and death of the young.

She took a moment to reflect on the pastor's challenge. Kwamboka tried to live her life as best she could and that was enough assurance for her. "There will be a judgment," she replied. Okemwa waited for more. "The meek shall inherit the earth. I believe that," she added. "If you didn't believe that the good people will win in the end, it would be hard to go on, don't you agree?"

"Yes, of course." Okemwa picked up a piece of buttered bread and smacked his lips as he chewed. "So, professor," he continued, changing the subject, "why don't you come to church more often? There's a place for you."

"There's just enough room for your parishioners as it is. I will make it one too many."

"I could only wish that were true. With you there, not only will the church be filled, it will become the first mega-church in Kisii," he said with a smile. Okemwa, like all the church ministers in Kabungu, knew that many parents would follow Kwamboka to the church and he was eager for her association and for the bounty that was sure to follow. Kwamboka wished Okemwa well but knew that the distinction of becoming Kisii's largest church would most likely fall on Sweet Chariot Resurrection Ministries with its charismatic and younger leader, Finlay Abuga. "I come to your office more than you appear in church. The last time I saw you there was . . ."

"When Zion's grandchild was baptized," she said.

"Yes. That was what, three years ago?"

Kwamboka laughed.

"More, I should say. She is now in Standard Four at Malaika."

"Time goes by quickly." He added, "All the more reason to get on the right side with Jesus."

She thought about Zion, who had started life as a Catholic then when her husband Edward Otundo died, she joined Kennedy Okemwa's church and when her thirty-year-old grandson established his own church, she went over to the church that brimmed with song, clapping, shouts and exuberant movements. That's when she dropped her first Christian name, Victoria, the name given to her at her infant baptism and adopted the self-chosen 'Zion.' About a year ago, she had returned to Okemwa's AICCD; to her grandson's dismay.

Kwamboka looked at Pastor Okemwa, slightly annoyed at his attempts to get her to join his church, then smiled tightly. She hadn't been a churchgoer since leaving Kenya to study and teach abroad. Her faith turned away from institutions and became more inward. Having come to age at the end of the colonial era, she was part of the generation that believed that Christianity was brought by the European gun. She no longer prayed and felt no need for the healing power that the churches offered. Her longing wasn't for God but for a rootedness that had eluded her.

****

14 Feb. 2009

WHILE HER HOUSE HAD ELECTRICITY, Sarah Kwamboka had only one small light, on her bed-stand. Televisions were

he area, yet she refused to buy one.
urbed nights where she could hear
neighbouring farms, the croaking of
of dogs. Lucy had encouraged her to
had been a rash of night-time house
laughed at the thought. No one would
want to bother her. There was nothing worth taking.

"They would just steal the dog," she said, ignoring the fact that her few possessions were valuable—far more than what most of her countrymen had. But compared to the judge's house in the valley or to that of the owner of the supermarket in town, or even those that were still under construction with rebar sticking up from the incomplete second stories, Kwamboka possessed little. Still, most homes in the area were little different from how they had been fifty years before and the lives of her neighbours not much improved since independence.

Nothing was taken on the night of the murder. The next morning, the boy who delivered milk to her door found a broken window and a shattered glass on the floor; the iron-gate that had been pried off the window lay bent beside the outside foundation. But nothing was ransacked, no drawers opened or clothes tossed on the ground. The few shillings Kwamboka had in the dresser were still where she had put them. Neither had the mobile phone been taken nor her laptop computer which was still on the kitchen table.

\*\*\*\*

### 21 Feb. 2009

A week before the funeral, when plans were still being made and Kwamboka's body lay in the mortuary, Inspector Dingiria approached Pastor Okemwa at his church office and asked for the opportunity to address the assemblage on the day of the eulogizing.

"This wasn't a robbery," Dingiria told the pastor. He was dressed neatly in civilian clothes, his shoulders a little too

broad for his cotton zipper jacket, the legs
trousers flapping around his thin legs. He was c
taller than Kennedy Okemwa.

Okemwa didn't register surprise by the inspector's c
"There are a hundred rumours about the killing," the past
said.

"Rumours aren't good. They fan the flames of violence,"
Sergeant Dingiria said. "No good comes from vigilantes let
loose by wild stories."

The comment irritated Okemwa. There is no justice
without vigilantes, he thought to himself. And he didn't put
much stock in facts. The police had no incentive to solve
crimes. Most murders remained notations on the police
blotter. Kwamboka's murder, however, was big enough to
call in a detective, so perhaps there was some hope that
this time it would be different.

"Sungusungu . . ." James Dingiria began.

"Do you think this is their work?" Okemwa interrupted,
surprised by the suggestion that the gang that was
terrorizing parts of the Kisii area was behind the murder.
Originally formed with the explicit encouragement of
the government as a grassroots way of fighting crime,
corruption and witches, there was an about-face when the
group could no longer be controlled and Sungusungu was
banned. Yet everyone knew that it continued to operate
with impunity, as the Administration Police were either
incapable or uninterested in reining it in. Armed with crude
weapons, Sungusungu looted and burned down houses
before lynching those they considered criminals. From talks
with well-placed congregants, Okemwa was convinced that
the police approved of Sungusungu. They were doing the
job that they themselves couldn't do.

Initially, Kennedy Okemwa also believed that Sungusungu
was an effective deterrent against the soaring crime rate in
the area. If the police were impotent, then someone else had

to step in. Lately, though, Sungusungu operated more like gangsters than protectors.

The beheading of three men at Nyanchwa outside Kisii Town had gone too far, Pastor Okemwa preached one Sunday morning. Criminals should be punished, "But," he said, "Christians shouldn't behead anyone, no matter how wicked." Unlike other sermons about the need for justice and beseeching of God's good graces to be bestowed upon the nation, his words were without conviction; he had no alternative proposal as to how to put a stop to the crime wave of house robberies, carjackings and rape cases that left many fearing that they were about to be tipped into hell.

"These young thugs are capable of anything," James Dingiria continued. "But this wasn't their work. First, they tie their victims' hands behind their backs. Second, they don't use guns. They bludgeon their victims to death. And third, they leave threats behind."

The inspector reached to the floor, picked up his briefcase and placed it on his lap.

This was the first time Okemwa met the CID sergeant, who had been brought in from another district. He wondered if the visit was a demand for a bribe.

Inspector Dingiria peered into his attaché case, moved aside a thick black folder and took out a single folded sheet of paper, the size of a letterhead.

"Here. Look at this," he said. "This is Sungusungu's signature. They always leave something like this behind. They want you to know it was them. They work by intimidation. There was nothing like this, was there?" he asked as he handed the pastor the flier with the bold lettering.

Okemwa unfolded the sheet of paper. He didn't need his glasses to see the large letters. He read it quickly. The pastor had seen several like it before, but not recently. So he shook his head and returned the flier to the inspector.

**CAUTION! CAUTION! CAUTION!**
**BODIES OF KILLED CRIMINALS**
**SHOULD BE BURIED AT THE**
**GOVERNMENT CEMETERY,**
**FAILURE TO, YOU WILL SUFFER**
**THE CONSEQUENCES.**
**THE REMAINING SHOULD**
**SURRENDER THEIR WEAPONS**
**AND THEMSELVES TO THE**
**NEAREST POLICE STATION AND**
**AREA CHIEF'S. WE KNOW YOU BY YOUR NAMES.**

"I didn't think so. What's more, there were only three. Sungusungu never operates in small numbers."

There had been rumours that the police had made an arrest, but this was the first time that anything official had been said.

"You've *caught* the murderers?" Okemwa asked just to make sure that he understood correctly.

"Yes," Dingiria said. "Three young men. They have been remanded in custody. They have confessed. Each of them."

Confessions: as a Christian minister he knew about their limitations. Confessions aren't always the full truth. A person admits to the least painful part—Oh, Lord, for I have sinned, forgive me for my trespasses. It is contrived to provide the greatest benefit with the least amount of candour. But it's the full truth that matters and what's in the heart. What was in these killers' hearts?

"And what did they say?"

"That they came to do a job and did it."

"That's all?"

Okemwa meant, 'is that all the evidence?' This may not be a real confession at all. It could be coerced; the police may have concocted it.

The detective went on to say that the noise of the break-in must have woken up Kwamboka who fumbled for her mobile phone. They found it on the far side of the bedroom; she must have dropped it, then kicked it as she hurried to find safety. There was no record of a call being placed. Her glasses were still beside the bed, on top of a book she had been reading. The light was off. She couldn't have seen the keys on the pad in the dark without her reading glasses.

Okemwa felt the throbbing in his temple. He placed his finger on the extended vein beside his left eye.

"We think she fled from her bedroom before they were fully inside. They found her locked behind the toilet door. They shot her right there," he said, pressing his forefinger on Okemwa's chest. "They left immediately but didn't take anything."

Okemwa placed his cold hands together and blew into the cup they had formed. The pastor then offered Sergeant Dingiria tea, which the inspector declined.

"Who is this Kombo woman?" the inspector asked abruptly, turning the conversation in a direction that unnerved the pastor.

"The first chairman of the Malaika School. She and Kwamboka founded it together," Okemwa said, swallowing some of his words.

The inspector jotted a note in his pad. He turned to the previous page.

"We found a file of papers in Kwamboka's house. On the top sheet was Lucy Kombo's name. Do you know why?"

Okemwa's gesture was ambiguous.

The detective reached into his briefcase again and produced the file. He handed the folder to the pastor who leafed through many pages. There were seven groups of papers, like chapters from a book. On each was a name.

"Yes, I think I know what this is." He told the sergeant that Kwamboka was interviewing people on stories about Kisii. Years ago, she had published a collection of folktales for young children. Now she had wanted something for the older ones. The note asked Lucy to review one of the stories she, Kwamboka, had finished writing.

"What kind of stories?" the inspector inquired.

Okemwa said that since Kwamboka had handed over her school responsibilities, she was interested in talking to people about their family stories.

"Like an anthropologist?" the inspector asked. "Or like a journalist?"

Okemwa thought about the distinction. It was difficult to answer. Kwamboka was neither. He recalled a conversation he had had with Kwamboka when she was beginning her inquires.

****

## 2006

"I'VE ALWAYS BEEN A PRESERVATIONIST," she said to the pastor, explaining to him why she was interested in collecting stories from the region. They were in Okemwa's house, the parsonage on the church property, a whitewashed building with red pantiles on the roof and curtains and tablecloths contributed by women congregants. Okemwa became a pastor when his wife died during a late-term miscarriage. He established the church a decade ago and had always lived in the house alone.

"In the 1960s I recorded Kisii folktales. My grandmother used to tell me tales at night before falling asleep. 'A story I am coming,' she always started. That's how I began the book."

"I've seen the book."

"It is in the Malaika library. I may have a copy in my home to give to you, if you like."

Okemwa nodded.

"I remembered the stories and then altered them slightly, so that others could understand them. I felt a little guilty, but, you know, we are always re-writing stories. But as long as you keep the spirit, it's all right. Now I am at it again, this time writing the stories from the lives of ordinary people in Kisii."

"Why Kisii?" Okemwa asked.

"We Abagusii don't know much about our past. Other parts of our country are well known, from newspapers and television shows. And just think about the books that are read in school. The government never seems to choose books about us to include in the curriculum, so there is so little about the area. Do you know of one Kisii poet or novelist, even one that mentions us?"

"There's you," he said.

"Not just for children. Do you know one Kisii who is known throughout the world besides our runners?"

Kwamboka didn't wait for a response. Okemwa knew that it was rhetorical.

"All we have are farms, with chickens and cows, a little coffee and some tea. No big stories about revolution. We haven't been lucky enough to have one of our own at the university who has connections with the publishers."

"That's true," the pastor said with a smile. He enjoyed Kwamboka's commitment.

"But everyone has a story that is worth telling and therefore worth preserving. I want to record this before tribal killings pull us all down."

"Amen to that, professor," the pastor said.

\*\*\*\*

### 21 Feb. 2009

"SHE SAID THAT?"

"She wanted to have a book about Kisii that would be used in schools. That was her dream."

"I mean about tribal killings pulling everyone down. Are you sure that is what she said?"

Okemwa hesitated.

"Pastor, please. Is that what she said?"

"I want to make sure I say only what she said. I don't want to put words in her mouth. So give me a moment. I want to get it right. Be accurate." He anxiously pulled at his beard. "Yes. That's what she said."

"Why do you think she would say such a thing?"

Was Dingiria baiting him? Every neighbour had bows and arrows in the household. Okemwa kept a hard wooden club under his bed. The church employed two night watchmen. Trade in shields and spears was brisk. In Kisii Town, offers for handguns were as common as solicitations by prostitutes.

Before Christmas 2007, just prior to the presidential election, Okemwa warned that Kenya could follow down the road of Rwanda's ethnic genocide or Amin dada's murderous paranoia. The local radio stations were vitriolic and politicians were handing out money to stage-manage demonstrations that would erupt in mayhem. And events nearly proved Okemwa a prophet: the post-election violence left shops smouldering in Kabungu. More than a dozen people were killed, some on the road, others in their homes. Entire families disappeared, their houses intact but empty. After calm was restored, Kennedy Okemwa's sermons turned more from charity to precaution—from Christian meekness to calls for God's justice.

"I can't say," Okemwa replied. He chose his words carefully. "I think what she meant was that we never know what tomorrow will bring."

"What we do know is that the funeral is next week. So let me get to the reason for my visit."

Okemwa thought that the inspector wanted background information about Kwamboka's investigation. Perhaps he did, but Dingiria said something unexpected.

"I want to address the gathering. With your permission. I know you will be the master of ceremonies. If you would be so kind, put me on the list of invited speakers. To quell the fears, give the news that the killers have been found."

The pastor explained that his role was to offer the opening prayer and introduce the others to make sure the program proceeded smoothly. He wasn't responsible for creating the list.

"Lucy Kombo is in charge."

The pastor was relieved with the turn in conversation. It was never a good thing to have the police ask you questions, especially in relation to a major crime. Okemwa silently thanked Jesus.

"Let me ring up Mrs. Kombo." Okemwa said he couldn't make the decision on his own. She was the person in charge, not he. He reached into his desk and took out his phone.

The detective nodded. Pastor Okemwa rang Lucy, but couldn't get a connection.

"I've run out of minutes on my card," said the inspector. "I have to buy some more."

"Here. Use mine." Dingiria handed him his own phone that he removed from his trouser pocket.

"Are you sure?"

Dingiria nodded.

The pastor quickly punched in Lucy's phone number on the inspector's mobile.

"No answer," Okemwa said after letting the phone ring for more than a minute. "But I'll take responsibility and say yes. I'm sure Lucy won't disagree," he said, hoping it was true.

Dingiria thanked the pastor. Before getting into his car, he asked Okemwa for the warning notice he had shown him and returned it to his briefcase. Dingiria straightened his gray rayon tie before getting into the car. As he sat behind the steering wheel, he leaned over to open the glove compartment to check for his pistol and, satisfied that it was there, put on his safety belt and drove back to police headquarters in Kisii Town.

# The Runner

## 28 Feb. 2009
## 10 A.M

GUY-ROPES OF THE LARGEST tent are tightened and final adjustments are being made on the reed roof over the newly constructed platform from which the speakers will talk. A boy in flip-flops is putting out bottles of water on tables in the nylon shelters where family and friends will be seated throughout the day.

There is a microphone in a stand and the cable is attached to a large black speaker, the one used for weekend dances at the Prestige Lakeside Club, the only dance hall in Kabungu. Static and squawking disturbs the soft voices engaged in conversation. The squeal sets a pair of birds in flight. Two men near the sound equipment are discussing a problem they seem to have. One gets into a Toyota pick-up truck to go to Kisii Town to find a technician who, they are sure, will get the balky equipment to cooperate. The driver signals his co-workers and they push the small red vehicle downhill. The driver releases the clutch and the truck bucks to a start.

Dingiria is wearing his uniform: blue pants, a shirt with his three stripes and a beret with his Criminal Investigation Division insignia.

A cluster of policemen stands by the church compound entrance. They are arranged in a loose circle, joking with one another, their batons tucked into their armpits. One wears a greatcoat, two have heavy cotton sweaters and six are in their short-sleeve shirts.

Lucy Kombo shakes hands with Rebecca Nyanchoka, an older woman wearing a woollen coat. Nyanchoka braces herself against a staff cinched with a silver ring on the shaft that is as tall as the bent *kizee*. Standing next to her but looking into the distance is Sweet Chariot Resurrection's pastor, Finlay Abuga.

Seeing the handsome minister, Dingiria looks at the program of the ceremony's speakers but the sun is so bright he finds that he must squint to read the small print. He moves to the shade under the portico of the AICCD social hall and consults his program. Abuga's name isn't on it. Dingiria notices that Abuga has placed his hand on a young woman's shoulder and he is talking to her. After a minute, Abuga leaves the woman—a congregant of his, Dingiria assumes— and walks over to several other smartly dressed women.

\*\*\*\*

### Feb. 21 2009

WHEN SGT. DINGIRIA LEFT the pastor's home, Okemwa walked to the general store and topped up his Safaricom call card. He phoned Lucy again. This time she answered. Okemwa talked to her as he walked rapidly along the verge of the busy road back to the parsonage. He put his hand to his ear to block out the noise of trucks grinding their gears as they lumbered up the incline.

"I don't know," Lucy said, responding to Okemwa's message regarding the inspector's desire to speak at the memorial service. "I think it is unseemly. The police have no place on the program."

The pastor thought otherwise. If the police were implicated in Kwamboka's murder or cover-up—"We don't know, Lucy. Nobody knows what happened." "Or ever will," Lucy added— it was best not to antagonize them.

"This time it might be different."

He could hear Lucy's snort. He didn't believe it himself. There was no reason to hope that the police would do their job and despite his trials to quell Lucy's cynicism, he knew that she was probably right.

"Let's not make things worse. No harm in meeting their request." Okemwa was running out of breath. He ducked into a lane off the road and leaned against a garden post. The valley, usually deep green with tea and pasture, was covered with a fine layer of dust and the ground where he stood was hard and strewn with rocks.

"Demand, you mean," she said.

"Call it what you will. It doesn't change things."

Lucy argued that it would be an insult to Kwamboka's memory to have a police spokesman address the mourners. Again, the pastor presented a different perspective, pointing out that there already were government representatives who were on the schedule. MPs, District Commissioners, District Officers, Chiefs and Assistant Chiefs were all on the program. Once Lucy had decided to broaden the speakers beyond the school community, there was no way to pare the list. No reason to unnecessarily antagonise the police, he argued.

"Everyone now wants to be seen as being on her side," Lucy said with resentment.

She conceded to Okemwa's entreaty. The inspector would speak at the proceedings.

****

## Feb. 19 2009

"DOES ANYONE KNOW LUCY KOMBO?" James Dingiria addressed those in the police station in town. Sunlight streamed in through the open casement window. "The one involved with the Malaika School for Little Angels. Kombo."

The three officers looked at him briefly, then returned to their work. The elderly clerk, Alfred Nyang'wara, stopped typing. A large, heavy hand of green bananas was propped against the cement wall and on Nyang'wara's desk was an empty coffee cup.

"I do," Nyang'wara finally said. The other officers stopped their work. The clerk was sweating under his woollen suit jacket frayed at the elbows. He envied Dingiria who wore a spotless shirt. "She was a friend to Sarah Kwamboka, the woman who was murdered."

"Yes, exactly," he said. "The one I am investigating. That's why I am asking. What can you tell me about her?"

Inspector James Dingiria's home was in Taveta, a town in the foothills of Mt. Kilimanjaro. He hadn't been in the Kisii region before being posted on temporary duty assignment for the Sarah Kwamboka investigation. James Dingiria graduated from the Kenya Police College and worked his way up the ranks of the uniformed police before he took additional courses at Kenyatta University and the Metropolitan Police Crime Academy in London before transferring to the CID. He knew that he would wind up in Kisii sooner or later: the area, the most densely populated rural part of Kenya, had a crime rate second only to Nairobi.

Until his recent re-assignment to Nyanza Province, all of Dingiria's postings had been in the dry Eastern province and along the Indian Ocean. He wasn't used to the high altitude or, despite the drought, the lushness that surrounded him, the greenness of it all.

Unlike his home that was occasionally visited for its nearby wildlife, Kisii was a kind of cul-de-sac. The only reason for a tourist to come this way was to visit the stone carvers at Tabaka, but this was a rare occurrence. Beyond Kisii Town were small places—Suneka, Rongo, Sare and Suba Kuria—before Isibania at the Tanzania border. Truckers and traders but few others had a reason to come to the rucketing Kisii Town, 70,000 people stuffed into a valley. Dingiria felt as if every person in Kenya had been squeezed into the suffocating half-mile downtown—people out on the main road or in the municipal market, in shops, in bars and hotels, a stinking town with no sewers, the air filled with the fumes of diesel buses, trucks and cars, a place layered with red mud from daily rains, where cows competed with crows for sugar cane husks strewn in the streets, an arrhythmic heart beating in the midst of what Dingiria conceded was Kenya's most beautiful countryside.

"When the Malaika School was started . . ." the elderly clerk began.

"When was that?" the inspector interrupted.

"The year of the first multi-party election," Nyang'wara said sharply.

"1992, you mean?"

"Yes. Kwamboka lived with someone named Malaika. It's the same house."

"She was . . .?" Dingiria asked.

"Who? Malaika?"

"Yes, that one."

Nyang'wara face heated and he sat up straight. "A young woman who owned a sewing shop. She called herself Malaika, after the popular song. Men loved her. That's the only name she went by. She made dresses for many of the women here."

"What was her name of record? And what happened to her?"

Dingiria was more officious than he wanted to be, but was unable to stop himself. He felt out of place and unwelcome, aware of the other officers listening to the conversation. Bad blood existed between CID officers and uniformed police throughout the country—their training was different, as were the chains of command. The CID was an elite force and for that reason resented by local police units. Being a newcomer to Kisii made Dingiria's presence more difficult than usual in the police headquarters.

He took a step back from Nyang'wara's desk.

"Rose Nyansarara." The clerk added, "And she died."

"Of what?"

"An illness." Malaria, pneumonia, tuberculosis, AIDS. Take your pick in Kisii.

"She convinced Kwamboka to start a school for girls."

"She *convinced* Kwamboka?"

The sergeant rubbed the lobe of his right ear between his forefinger and thumb.

"It caused a lot of turmoil at the time" the clerk said, feeling intimidated by this stranger's interrogation. A CID inspector could make his life miserable. "A lot. People didn't trust Kwamboka, but some did. The headmaster of the government school threatened her. A Mr. Ondari. But then Kwamboka became more popular with the people. They saw the school was good and she was honest. No one could bribe her. So people came to trust her and some even wanted her to run for a political office."

"Which she did not, I assume." Dingiria filled in the thought.

"No. She didn't join *Maendeleo wa Wanawake* either."

"Wouldn't that have made her stronger, being part of the national women's group?"

The clerk continued cautiously, "Who knows? Maybe she wanted to be independent. I don't think she ever wanted to be a strong person. *Maendeleo* was big here at the time. But it also became part of the government. She was asked but she didn't join."

"People must have resented her," the inspector asserted. "Rejecting the political party that way."

He took a seat next to Nyang'wara. He picked up the empty coffee mug. "Is there any more coffee?"

Nyang'wara looked around. The two administrative policemen at the nearby desk didn't move. The clerk pulled the sheet of paper from his typewriter, put it in his centre desk drawer, got up, went to the next office and returned a few minutes later with a coffee pot, another cup and saucer, and a small bowl of sugar on a tray. He poured the coffee for Dingiria. The inspector noisily pulled a chair across the room to sit next to the clerk.

"Tell me about Lucy Kombo," Dingiria asked. "She and Kwamboka started the school. And they always got along?"

"Yes. They were very good friends."

"Kombo is married?"

The clerk said that her husband was Dennis Kombo. He was confined to his farm. He had been a trucker but was forced out of work when he was blinded in one eye.

"An accident?"

"A misunderstanding," the clerk responded.

"A fight, then," Inspector Dingiria said.

Nyang'wara said that Kombo was a brave man, but even brave men can be afraid.

One of the other officers intervened.

"I know him," the policeman said, talking to Dingiria from across the room. "Kombo was a truck driver but he never took foolish chances."

Dingiria went over to him and sat down. The officer explained that Kombo followed the law: the vehicle had the proper inspections, his license was up-to-date, and he was polite to other drivers on the road and never argued with the police. He was also careful. Like most drivers, he kept an iron bar under the seat of the cab, just in case. Many vehicles were hijacked, especially ones that were carrying goods that could be sold on the black market.

Why is he volunteering all this information? Dingiria wondered.

"He is a cousin of mine," he said, as if reading the inspector's thoughts. Clearly he wanted to present Kombo in a good light.

On one of his trips, the officer continued, to Mwanza, in Tanzania, Kombo heard a story that was confirmed in the *Nation* the day after a fellow trucker related it to Kombo in a Tarime bar over bottles of Pilsner. This was different than the often-related one: As trucks were lined up a half-mile waiting for customs officials to examine documents, add their stamps to custom papers, rifle through goods and be given their unofficial bonuses—the common story went—a driver was pulled from the cab of his truck by hijackers who stole both his truck and his manhood, which was stuffed in his trouser pocket. Everyone laughed no matter how often the tale was repeated; it was close enough to the truth that they could feel frightened but shrug it off with bravado by ridiculing the neutered driver. But something did happen that was true. One of the truckers came to a roadblock and pulled to the side of the road for the usual inspection of registration and license. No other vehicles were nearby. He rolled down the window of his cab when the police put a gun against his head and shot him dead. This wasn't another example of bad police behaviour.

"Then what?" Dingiria asked.

"They were criminals dressed up as policemen," the officer said. "So when Kombo was coming back from Tanzania and got to a police check a few miles on the Kenya side before the border crossing, he didn't stop. He ran through it. But it really *was* the police this time. They shot at the truck. A bullet went through the windscreen. This is how he became blind in one eye. Kombo couldn't drive after that," the officer concluded. "He devoted himself to his farm and helped Lucy with her endeavours at the school. He worked on the school's construction and often helped out with cleaning the property. In the last few years he has been confined to the farm."

If the Inspector wanted to talk to Kombo, the officer said, he was sure he could find him at his farm, a small plot of land with a patch of pyrethrum, the crop he decided to keep instead of ripping it up and planting tea, as did most of his neighbours. There was more money in tea, but Lucy preferred the small white flowers to the tea bushes, and Kombo was happy to please her.

Dingiria thanked the clerk and the officer for their help. They didn't acknowledge him. The clerk put the paper back in the typewriter and the officer sat silently with his colleague.

Dingiria poured himself a second cup of coffee and carried it to the desk next to the open window. Before sitting down, he took a deep breath. The noisome air outside was better than the staleness inside. Dingiria took out the pile of papers, Kwamboka's manuscript, from the desk drawer where he had put it after taking it from her house. He didn't know if the stories should be read in the order in which he found them. He didn't know if Kwamboka had ordered them for a reason or whether they had been arranged randomly. There was also no indication which parts of the stories she had simply recorded and which parts were fabricated and imagined. Because of the conversation he had just, he decided to read Dennis Kombo's story first.

\*\*\*\*

*The garden at the Kisii Hotel was the place to be. Today, with all the building going on, there are dozens of places to enjoy a drink with friends. I can't keep up with all the changes. I'm certain there is a new spot opened every day where the up-and-comers meet one another. I once cared about such things, but I'm far too old for that now. Today I'm happy to have a beer with a friend in my house. I don't need to be seen.*

*Perhaps it is because of my age that I look back and think those were better times. Nostalgia is one of the curses of the elderly. But can anyone really enjoy all this crowding and noise? It seems like every time I come to Kisii Town and even here in Kabungu, there is new construction underway, and you can hardly get from one side of the street to the other because there are so many cars, trucks and buses that clog the way. I wonder when the name will be changed from Kisii Town to Kisii City.*

*The story I am going to tell you took place when I was still a youngster, before I couldn't stand to work in an office anymore and became a truck driver. We would often gather chairs from around the garden and bring them to our table. We never knew how many of us would be there, so we would take chairs from all over and bring them to our table. But the chairs weren't ours. We didn't own them. If anyone asked for an empty chair, we were obliged to give it up, even if we were waiting for another friend. This was the custom. It was always sociable there and everyone got along with us, even if we sometimes got too drunk for our own good.*

*My friends and I gathered here every Saturday afternoon to welcome the weekend. The usual group consisted of Ronald, Francis, Eunice, Jennifer and I. Eunice worked at the bakery and Jennifer at the photography shop on the main street. The two men worked in accounts at local businesses.*

*We remained at our small wooden table until late at night or until we were chased inside by heavy thunderstorms that blow in from the lake almost every evening. As soon as the rain stopped, we would go outside again and continue having our good time.*

*Some friends liked other hotels better, such as the Safe Lodge, because it is right in the town centre. Francis preferred the Mwalimu Hotel near the post office because it was newer. I was also partial to that hotel because the teachers' union owned it and I felt a bit of sympathy for teachers and wanted* to support them. But when you went to the Mwalimu hotel, you had to sit at the bar inside the building since there is no garden at that hotel. As a bookkeeper at the County Council, I felt stuffy being inside an office most of the day. I would go outside whenever I could during lunch hours, so I preferred the Kisii Hotel to any other. I looked forward to sitting at a table outdoors where I could take off my shoes and feel the grass under my bare feet. It reminded me of the time when I lived for running. This was long before Kisii became world-famous, except for the old man,  Mogaka, because of the professional runners- the ones who win the middle-distance races all over the world these days.

I know that at my prime I was never as good as they are today. Now they have all the advantages. They have trainers; they attend running schools and make lots of money. But I think that along with Nyandika Maiyoro, I made it possible for them to be where they are. I followed the  Mogaka and they followed me.

There were many bottles of Pilsner and White Cap on the table when someone we had never seen before came over.

"Excuse me," the stranger said so softly that I could hardly hear. He bowed slightly from his waist, the way I've seen some waiters do in expensive restaurants in Nairobi. I couldn't tell how old he really was, but he didn't look any older than we were. I'm sure my friends had seen thin bones like his only on Maasai's and Samburu's. (Remember this was maybe forty years ago.) He was wearing a white shirt that was so bright it almost hurt my eyes. He had on dark trousers and was wearing sandals, so you could see the toes of his white socks sticking out the opening in the front. His night-dark eyes matched the colour of his long straight hair, which fell limply around his ears.

"Excuse me," he said again. "Is anyone using this chair?"

Ronald hadn't seen him approach us; he hadn't heard him

the first time, his voice was so faint. Ronald turned to see who was standing beside us.

"What?" Ronald asked sharply, as this man had interrupted our lively conversation.

The stranger spoke with an unfamiliar accent, making it twice as difficult to clearly understand his request. There are always foreigners at the hotel at that time, from Europe mostly, people on aid missions in the western part of the country. There weren't many other places in Nyanza where foreigners were willing to lodge those days. I guess it isn't so different today. This worn hotel was the best there was to offer. We didn't mind the place but visitors did. Still, the wazungu's wouldn't think of staying at the Mwalimu or the Safe lodge Hotel. I don't know why, but that's the way it was. They thought this hotel was the best of the lot. Maybe because they could stay outside, like we did, away from the smell of toilets. So it wasn't surprising to find a few wazungu's here now and then. But this young man wasn't European or African.

Ronald was really annoyed. I don't think he understood what the young man was asking or why he was bothering us. But I understood. I recognized the accent immediately. And I could also tell something about him just from his look— the colour of his skin, the shape of his eyes, his hair, it all seemed familiar to me. It made me feel uncomfortable. Like Ronald, I also wished the stranger could go away.

"Excuse me, the chair is empty," the stranger said, as if we didn't know that. "No one is using it. Can I take it, please?"

Francis said to the stranger, "A friend is coming."

The young man stood next to us and looked very uncomfortable. A smile revealed his polished teeth. He waited quietly for permission to take the chair.

I leaned over to Francis and whispered to him in Gusii. "Let him have it."

*The young man smiled and bowed again. He didn't know what I was saying.*

*"Martha said she would be here," Eunice chided me. "Don't give it to him." She says this in English, but I could tell that the stranger didn't understand her. He is having a hard time understanding our English as we did his.*

*Now Jennifer joined in. "All the chairs are taken," she said, looking up at the stranger. "Go into the bar. There are spaces there for you."*

*Her comment and Francis' made me feel something in my stomach because they weren't being honest about this. If Martha did show up, one of us would have squeezed over and we would have doubled-up on the wooden chairs. We did that many times and no one ever minded. The table could never be too crowded for companions. In fact, the closer together we pressed, the more enjoyable it became. So I ignored Jennifer's remark.*

*"Take it," I said to him, surprised by my own boldness in contradicting my friends. They all looked at me. "It isn't being used right now."*

*He thanked us, bowed again and carried the chair to the far end of the garden where he sat by himself near the bamboo. I wondered what he was doing here—maybe business. Maybe he was a student. I began to think about him. The first bottles of beer were drained for the afternoon and we ordered more.*

*"Who was that?" Ronald asked. "Is he a friend of yours?"*

*Francis laughed at Ronald's teasing.*

*"Someone who needs a seat," I said. "You aren't deaf, are you? You heard what he said." I said this a little harshly.*

*"No one can understand him. What language was that?"*

*"English," I said. "It's English."*

"He is a funny looking one," Jennifer said scornfully. "I have never seen anyone like that before."

"He looks like he›s sick." Eunice now joined the chorus of complains. "He looks yellow. Instead of giving him the chair we should take him to a hospital and give him blood."

The young man didn›t look sick to me. That›s just how they look when they come from that part of the world. But I know why she said that. When I first went to China, I thought the same thing. I didn›t like much about China—the way the people smelled, the way they always smiled, the food, the cold winters, the hot summers, the throngs of people in the shops, the sky so filled with factory smoke that my nose was always clogged with big chunks of dirt.

Everyone laughed at the jokes about this man that were flying around the table. I did not find this funny, though.

I think strangers should always be welcome. I know what it›s like to be away from home and not have people invite you to be part of their group. It›s no fun at all. But I didn't say anything. I kept my mouth shut, although what was said hurt me. Francis and I should have known better.

I am ashamed of myself even when I think about it today. It reminds me of what we used to say about others in Kenya— that they were too dark, that their noses were too broad and their faces too round, or that they were too tall, short or skinny.

Francis had once lived in England. I could excuse the others. They hadn't been any further than Nairobi, or maybe Mombasa once. They hadn't even been to Uganda. They had never been anywhere where they would be strangers, not know how to talk properly or be familiar with the customs there. But Francis and I shouldn›t have acted that way. We had the good fortune to receive scholarships. And I knew what it›s like being able to speak only to myself for months at a time.

*I don,t want to think about all this. It was long ago and I am happy to forget about my experience. Unlike Francis, I couldn't chat about it with my friends over food or use it to impress women. The food I ate in China I,ve never seen in Kisii or anywhere else in Kenya, not even at the coast. Half the time I had no idea what was on my plate. If I asked about this or that thing on the table, the other students would smile at me but not answer. I ate it because if I didn,t I would starve to death. Even the tea wasn,t like the tea we drink— they had no milk, no sugar and it was yellow, not black.*

*When I first returned home, everyone wanted to know about being a runner at a foreign university, who I ran against, what prizes I had been awarded. I talked about the various contests and all the records I held. Little by little, I stopped talking about it until no one asked any more. Today it is history. That day, watching that Asian man sitting alone in this garden bursting with people laughing and telling each other stories, I was very quiet. I was remembering the days as a runner and it seemed as though I was there, young again and running in China as fast as a gazelle.*

*As a youngster when I thought about what my life would be like as an adult, I thought about    Mogaka, Nyandika Maiyoro, the great runner from Kiogoro, Nyaribare Chache. He was the first East African to be represented in the Commonwealth Games. This was in Vancouver, Canada, in 1954. He finished fifth in the five mile, because he started the race two laps late. He did not understand English and his coach, a Mr. Evans, had gone for a short call moments before the start of the race. Evans convinced organizers to allow him to take part and Maiyoro, running barefoot, chased the runners like a hunter going after an antelope, as whites wondered, «What is this baboon up to?» Back home, the colonial officers, persuaded by Chief Musa Nyandusi, built a four-bedroom house for him inside the Gusii Stadium. He ran many times on the world stage, and he retired after the 1964 Olympic Games, before I was getting started.*

*Everyone here respected him since he was the first black Kenyan to be known around the world and he was a Kisii. Every boy from Kisii found inspiration in his accomplishments. He was the pride of us all. His life was the one I wanted for myself. I couldn't think of anything better than to organize sporting events for the district the way he was doing at that time. I hoped that Kisii Town Council would build a house for me and I would be the next to take up his residence in the small flat under the stands at the stadium, the stands that filled with people enjoying themselves and cheering and it all taking place right above my own head, right outside the door of my very own home.*

*Father Therkettle was the running coach at my school. Of course I knew about our famous runner, but something else really made me want to become a track star. It was something Father Therkettle did. One day, he showed us a movie in the classroom. He told us to watch it closely, that we would see something wonderful in it. I had no idea what it was at first. But then I saw that it was about the American runner called Jesse Owens. On the track next to him was a horse and when the starter's gun cracked, Owens jumped from the blocks and crossed the finish line before the horse. The next part of the movie showed this same black American marching in front of the viewing stand during the Olympic Games in Germany. Father Therkettle explained how the German dictator, Hitler, left the stadium rather than watch the black man receive a medal after winning the race. This was even worse than when the British were here.*

*So I practiced every day, in the morning when the grass was wet with dew and every evening, often on a muddy field. Others stayed inside when black clouds came overhead and there was lightning, but nothing could keep me from practice until I couldn't stand up any longer. It was as though I had become infected with a fever. I had no doubt that one day I would be the fastest runner to come out of the Kisii highlands. I knew that my family would be honoured by my success and everyone in Kenya would know me.*

*There was a map that hung on the wall in my classroom. It was one of the old ones from before independence. Africa was filled with green and pink and gray—French, British and independent. I looked at the map all the time and plotted how I would run across Africa. I could see myself running along the thin red lines on the map, around blue lakes and across the Sahara. I looked at the equator line that cut Kenya into two, right there by Kisumu, and I wondered if it was different running north of the equator. I thought, Should I first go north to Sudan then west across the forests of the Belgian Congo and then to green Equatorial Africa and finally to the blue Atlantic Ocean? Or should I run south to another pink place, Tanganyika, and then to the Indian Ocean? I studied the map intently, memorizing the names of the cities along the way, imagining how I would be greeted as I ran along. Everyone would stand outside his house and watch me. This is how I learned geography. But at that time it never occurred to me that in many of those places, even right here in Africa, no one could speak Gusii, or Swahili, or even English—the three languages I knew at the time. Only now I realize that running through Africa could be as lonely as being in China.*

*The waiter brought our first round of samosas on a small white plate. We ate these fried little meat pies as fast as they arrived. We were still waiting for the chips ordered by Francis. He always ordered chips. He's the only one who did.*

*"In England, they wrap fish and chips in old newspapers," he told me more than once. We have to hear it again because of the women who have joined us, although I'm certain they have also heard it before.*

*Francis is a bookkeeper, at the coffee union by the river at the other end of town. His uncle was one of the members of the board of trustees there and got the position for Francis.*

*The chips arrived.*

"They fry the fish in batter—milk and flour," he continued to explain the strange manners of the British. "The potatoes are made in a pot of boiling oil."

"I think if we squeeze these chips, we get all the oil out again," Ronald said, looking at the greasy serviette. "It is enough to use in my car."

Jennifer ordered a cup of coffee.

Even though we never ordered chips ourselves, we always ate what the waiter brought to Francis. He tried to persuade the hotel manager to make fish for a snack to go with our afternoon pombe. This has never happened. Maybe it requires too much work for a snack in a beer garden. Or maybe it's because the cook, who was a very big man but mute, didn't want to be bothered with snacks as well as meals. I knew that he could prepare battered fish, though. A few times, at night, we had gone into the dining room to have a meal where we ate fish.

"The chips in England are much better," Francis said as he licked his fingers. I think that if Francis had been served fried shit in England he would have said he liked that too.

Francis had been a good friend since we went to secondary school together. I understood why he talked about the UK. His scholarship to study bookkeeping in England had come as a great surprise to him. An association there offered to sponsor one person from the coffee union for two months at a special school for co-operatives. After graduating from secondary school, he had given up hope of studying abroad. Every student hoped that he would be selected to study in a foreign country. Of course, very few ever went. Before our time there were more scholarships available. If you graduated from secondary school in the 1950s, a college in America or in communist Europe wanted to give you a scholarship. I heard of someone who even went to Hungary. And I've known some who went to India and Norway, but no one from our school, other than me, ever received such a *scholarship when our time came. So I knew how important England was to Francis, what an honour it was to have gone to study in Europe after having graduated from school.*

When Father Therkettle told me that I was good enough to be a star runner, I knew he was right. The Standard had mentioned me more than once and the Daily Nation referred to me as a prospect for a future All-Africa Games. I dreamed that I would be remembered in the circle with the great Kipchoge Keino and others, like the old man at the stadium. I knew that Keino had been a police officer and had trained in Kenya. So I thought that after I graduated from secondary school I would also enter the police force to get training. But that isnʋt what happened. Instead, I received an offer from China. I had never thought of going to China before, but I couldnʋt resist the chance. Father Therkettle asked me to think about it carefully. He knew nothing about the college that offered the scholarship and he had no idea about their track program.

"Indeed," he said, "I suspect they do not have one." And he questioned whether it was wise for me to go there. The letter from the Chinese Embassy in Nairobi inquired after my grades. They wanted to know if I could succeed in a rigorous academic program. I wasnʋt the most clever boy at school, but no one had a doubt that if I applied myself to my studies equal to my running, I would do well enough.

"You can go, if you choose," Father Therkettle assured me, as we walked across the football field, his arm across my shoulder. At that moment I thought of that man, Jesse Owens. "But I donʋt know if it will be the best for you."

I thought that maybe he didnʋt want me to go because of China being a communist country. Everyone knew that communism wasnʋt a good thing. They didnʋt believe in God, most of all. And look at what has happened in Tanzania. I didnʋt want any part of socialism. At this time, though, world politics had already changed. So what if China was a supporter of Oginga Odinga, the disgraced vice-president from Luoland.

I considered the priest's advice. I respected him. But it didn't take me long to decide. How could being in the police be better than getting a university education? How could going to Central Province right here in Kenya be better than going to China, someplace that no one I knew had ever been to before? If being a policeman was so good, I could always become one when I returned. How could wearing boots all the time be better than running free up and down hills?

We finished our next round of pombe. Brown bottles, the labels peeling off, were strewn all around the garden—under the tables, on the grass; everywhere. Now there was hardly an empty spot at the hotel, either outside or at the bar in the lobby, it was so crammed full.

"Hey, Jennifer," Ronald said, "I'm going to come by on Monday to have you snap my photo."

"Oh, oh. I'll get a camera with stronger lens; I don't want you breaking it with your ugly face."

"Look who's talking! See what you can do for her, Eunice, to brighten her up a little, will you? You know, a proper dress . . ."

Chattering filled the evening air; every table was packed with men and women unwinding after the long week. And at the garden's far end sat the young man who had come to our table to borrow a chair. I looked at him. He was still alone. No one had joined him. He didn't even sit at a table but had his chair near the flowerbed not far from the room with the folding screen where other people ate dinner. But he looked absorbed in his reading, indifferent to the parties around him. Maybe he was waiting for a friend. Maybe he was waiting for a business associate or someone else from work. I didn't know. I didn't know why he was here or where he was from.

"Dennis," I heard Francis say, as though calling me from some far off place. But I could hardly understand him, thinking as I did about another country, another time.

To this day I can smell it, the aroma of garlic on everyone's breath and the factory smoke that made my nostrils cake with smoke. The only thing that reminded me of home was the smell of burning charcoal. I remember not being able to get warm in winter. During my two years in Shenyang Polytechnic Institute, in that big city in Manchuria, I set all kinds of records. Not only was I the best at Poly; I was the provincial middle-distance champion. The more I ran, the bigger the crowds at the Institute stadium, a huge facility in which 40,000 or more came to watch a competition. It was the biggest stadium I had seen until that time. I ran to the roar of cheering students and famous politicians who came to see me whiz past every other runner. The better I ran, the more they cheered. They had banners with my name on them, even one in English letters so I could read it. They chanted my name. «Kombo! Kombo! Kombo!»

When I won and ran around the track, it was like nothing I ever thought possible. One of the newspapers interviewed me and I was featured on a television show. It was amazing, something wonderful.

But this rush, like pombe drunk too quickly, didn't last long. Little by little the thrill disappeared and by the end of the year it had been completely replaced by resentment. On the track I was Number One Hero, inspiration to the proletariat, someone whose diligence was to be imitated by the worker in the automobile factory. But off the track I was something else completely. No one talked to me. If they could avoid it, they would even ignore a question from me. My roommates shunned me and in the cafeteria no one came to sit with me during meals. Between semesters, when many students left to go home or work with a brigade, I remained almost alone in campus. No one invited me to his home. I never met a Chinese family or saw the inside of any house.

*I had only one friend. He was a runner from another college far across the city. We took a streetcar to see one another. Ali was from Zanzibar, a communist outpost at the time, and as far as I knew he and I were the only two Africans in this city. Sometimes we went for a walk in a park or sat together outdoors on a bench if it wasnِt too cold. But Ali and I noticed something strange every time we got together. We thought that someone was following us. Every time we went to a teashop or even a restaurant we noticed the same Chinaman watching us. We were sure that he was a government spy, although neither of us could imagine what danger he thought we posed to the country. So after a short while, whenever we got together, we spoke only in Swahili, in part because it was sweet to hear a familiar tongue but also just in case he could overhear us he would have a hell of time figuring out what we were saying. In truth, we were frightened of being thrown into prison. Many students disappeared, either killed or sent to a distant part of the country.*

*In a short time, we realised that the government didnِt think we were spies but something worse. We both became aware that our fellow students ignored us all the time whenever we approached them. Everyone was afraid of us. Everywhere around campus were stories (rumours, we called them) that African students in Shanghai, more than a thousand miles away, had raped Chinese women at a college party. The Chinese men at the polytechnic said that Africans wanted only to have sex with Chinese women and that at every party attended by Africans there were riots. They said Africans were savages, barbarians, uncivilized, shenzi we would say in Swahili. I couldnِt defend myself since I hadnِt been accused of anything personally. My crime was being African. I was a criminal because I was black. Whenever I walked down a hall way in college, the women ran into their rooms, terror stricken, as though I were a witch.*

*One day, I heard someone call me a "black devil." I grabbed him tight at the neck of his shirt and banged his head against the wall. At least that is what I wanted to do to him.*

*Ali chose to stay in Shenyang to finish his degree. He didn,t want to jeopardize his chances for promotions at home. If he gave up this college, he said he would never get a degree elsewhere and a poor man without a degree would remain poor all his life, especially in Tanzania. He was right about the opportunity that would be lost if I came home before earning my degree. I knew I should have done the same as Ali and remained. It was foolish to leave the polytechnic because of the insults I received. But I couldn,t stay. I hated it too much. Neither would I join the police upon returning home. My taste for running had been spoiled, like being poisoned by rotten food and being in China. I had enough of the police as I ever would want for the rest of my life.*

*Eunice was talking about wanting to go to Kisumu the next day and Ronald went on about a song from Zaire he had heard on the radio. Francis finished his chips. Martha arrived and squeezed onto the chair with Jennifer.*

*I looked across the garden. The stranger with the strange hair folded the magazine he had been reading and put it into his jacket pocket. We were still having a fine time as he walked by.*

*He stopped at our table and bowed to us again.*

*"Thank you," he said to us as he continued to walk through the hallway of the hotel to the car park.*

*"Who is that?" Martha asked.*

*"No one," Francis said.*

*I wanted to talk to Francis and remind him what it was like being a stranger in a foreign land. I knew that if I didn't say anything to him I would be ashamed of myself. But I never did . And now it is too late.*

# African Marigolds

28 Feb. 2009

11 A.M.

THE LAWN THAT STRETCHES from the church to the roadway fills with people, as multicoloured-panelled parasols are opened under the cloudless sky, the assembly of policemen shifting from foot to foot, their vans parked on the roadside at the bottom of the hill. Lucy Kombo and dignitaries from Nyanza Province are sheltered under the tent set up to the side of the gleaming building of African Independent Church of Christian Disciples.

Kennedy Okemwa walks back to the church, while Pastor Abuga sits under a small nylon shelter engaging in a lively conversation with several women.

Inspector James Dingiria stands apart from the other police officers. He is under the shade of a blue gum tree watching the comings and goings on the platform that is now readied for the funeral speakers. A crocheted cloth covers the table and a vase of lilies is placed in the centre.

Lucy has compromised with Dingiria's request to speak at the service. He will address the guests, but it won't be in the early afternoon, in the middle of the service, but later, the last in the line of representatives from the administration who are programmed on the schedule. The detective was going to be scheduled where she wanted him or he wouldn't speak at all. Dingiria knows that many will have drifted away by the time he addresses them, but that doesn't matter a great deal. He has no doubts that what he has to say would be spread quickly and by the next day everyone would be aware of his remarks.

A technician walks up the hill. The pick-up remains parked outside the church compound, the traffic too thick to get through and the police unwilling to make way for it. Lucy talks to him when she sees him. The technician walks to the pile of equipment, pushes levers on the equalizer, plugs the microphone wire into one outlet, then another in the amplifier, changes the batteries in the portable microphone and turns dials on yet another piece of equipment. He taps the microphone to see if it is working. It is. He then tests the cordless microphone. It, too, is in working order.

****

## 20 Feb. 2009

SGT. INSPECTOR JAMES DINGIRIA TOOK Sarah Kwamboka's files from her home and began to read through them. Notes were attached to each story. One note, perhaps to herself, was an explanation of her project.

I want to preserve something about the Abagusii before we are absorbed into this new creation called 'Kenyan.' To remember is to honour our ancestors. And to honour them is to respect ourselves. Nothing good can come from forgetting our past. We can go forward properly only when we accept where we have come from, who we have been, what we have gone through. I put together these stories so those times and these people won't disappear like smoke from a fire but will stay like the aroma in the cooking house, feeding our hungry souls. These are 'true' accounts of people who have lived ordinary lives. In retrospect, we can see these were extraordinary times. Sometime in the future, someone will look back on us and say the same about us and the times in which we have lived.

Having read Dennis Kombo's story, Dingiria next chose to read a story that Lucy had narrated about her uncle Moseti. He was amused by the coincidence between Moseti's encounter with an Italian and something from his own life. At the police academy in England, he was assigned *On Crimes and Punishments* and was struck by the 18th century Italian author's name—Beccaria—and how it rhymed with his own. He laughed as he read Moseti's story and said to himself, *Il mio amico. Did you steal your name?*

Lucy and Kwamboka were contemporaries and had known each other since Kwamboka's return from her stay in America. Although Lucy and Dennis never had children themselves, Lucy helped Kwamboka establish the Malaika School for Little Angels. The two were fond of each other and over time Kwamboka and Lucy became close like sisters.

Kwamboka lived in the house beside the school that had been Malaika's. Lucy's home was closer to Sotik, in the area that had once been deemed off-limits to Africans, until the time of independence. This was a brilliant country, Dingiria thought, at least as good for its rich soil and beauty as the famed former White Highlands.

In order to understand why the post-election violence had erupted in the area, Dingiria read about the history of the district. He learned that the Kisii and Kipsigis both claimed the district as rightfully theirs. Numerous battles had taken place over centuries between the two groups and when the British arrived the area was designated as a buffer zone between the two tribes. The colonial government calculated that the white farmers would serve as a barrier to keep the Kisii and Kipsigis apart from one another and this became a region with a small number of European settlers. After independence, Kisii's and Kipsigis' bought land and were given title deeds.

The Kombo farm had been attacked several times in the last decade, as aggrieved Kipsigis hoped to intimidate the couple into abandoning their land. The Kombos had once received a note that read:

**THIS IS KIPSIGIS COUNTRY**

**LEAVE OR YOU WILL BE FORCED TO LEAVE**

**ALL KISII'S MUST GO BY THE 5$^{TH}$**

**NO EXCEPTIONS**

**THIS LAND BELONGS TO KIPSIGIS!!**

The threat didn't amount to anything. They ignored it and for a decade they lived peacefully with their neighbours. Until the recent election, that is. A day after the disputed results, her general store was burnt to the ground, as was the *posho* mill, the tailor shop and the primary school. For a month the Kombos housed four displaced tea pickers who fled from the plantations in Kericho to avoid being slaughtered.

When Dingiria went to the Kombos' home, he found Lucy's husband sitting on a folding chair in front of the concrete house with a roof of metal sheeting. Expecting a robust person in mind from "The Runner," Dingiria instead found an old man with clothes that hung loosely on his body and a face nearly expressionless, one eye shut closed. The former runner's receding hair was completely white. His right arm hung loosely at his side while he clutched a walking stick with his left hand. He stared at the neatly dressed policeman in civilian clothes and before he had a chance to apologize for his lack of hospitality, Lucy exited the house, a *kanga* wrapped around her waist and a kerchief covering her hair. She knew immediately who Dingiria was even though he was out of uniform. Okemwa had described him well.

"The pastor called me about you," she said coldly, dispensing with pleasantries. Lucy's high cheekbones reflected the sunlight. "Don't worry. You will be on the program."

Dingiria thanked her for obliging him.

"I want to talk to you, about Kwamboka, if I may" he added.

"You've already caught the murderers. I've heard that. What more is there?" she asked, hardly able to hide her contempt. Lucy believed that the police were useless. She knew what the outcome would be. The boys would be sentenced, the government would claim that justice had been done and the three would disappear forever.

"I want to know more about Kwamboka," he explained. "I know that the two of you started the Malaika School for Little Angels."

Lucy didn't offer a drink or a seat. The two stood by the door in the sun.

"We did."

"And that Rose Nyansarara, who was also known as Malaika, encouraged the two of you," Dingiria said flatly.

Kombo listened to the nearby conversation and struggled to follow it. Something about Malaika. He remembered flirting with her. What man in Kisii didn't? But it never bothered Lucy. She never questioned Dennis's love and loyalty to her. She once told him that she was the luckiest woman in the world to have him as a husband. His eyes began to well with tears as those words came back to him.

"This is a great loss," Lucy said. She put her hand on Dennis's shoulder when she noticed his tears. She wasn't surprised; lately he had become weepy at any mention of the past. "No one should die like this." Lucy hoped that she would be spared the details of the murder.

"Prof. Kwamboka was writing stories," Dingiria prompted.

"Yes, she was speaking to many people."

Dingiria asked Lucy to tell him more about Kwamboka, before she got involved with Malaika. Lucy began to soften. There was something about him that she trusted. Perhaps it was his training that taught him how to put people at ease or the lack of a uniform. Lucy found that she was willing to talk to him about her friend. Maybe she just needed to talk about Kwamboka.

She told him that Kwamboka had been a scholar, with degrees from the University of Nairobi and London.

"She was Dr. Kwamboka, but she didn't want anyone to call her that."

"She was modest?"

"Yes," she said. And no one wanted to become the object of someone's jealousy, she thought to herself.

Lucy said that Kwamboka taught in the United States, then returned to Kenya.

"Why did she come back?"

Lucy told him that the police had beaten her.

Dingiria raised his eyebrows. Lucy regretted having said this.

"Kwamboka told me it was because she was black."

Dingiria could believe such a story. It was consistent with America's reputation, at least until the election of Barack Obama.

Dingiria asked for more details.

There were demonstrators in a New York City park.

"What was she protesting?" Dingiria asked.

"She lived nearby and was walking home with her American friend, the one who sent money to the school." Lucy didn't like the implication that Kwamboka was responsible for what happened to her. "The demonstration became a riot. There was violence. She happened to be there when the police raided the park."

"This is what she told you?"

"Kwamboka had an article from a newspaper that had a photo of her with her face bloodied. She showed it to me."

Lucy didn't say that Kwamboka also had an article from a New York newspaper that said that the police were the ones responsible for having caused the riot and the brutality.

"Kwamboka said that at least in Kenya if you got in trouble, it would be because of choices you make, not anything as humiliating as the colour of your skin."

"And what choices were those?"

"Kwamboka only wanted to make the Malaika School for Little Angels the best school. This caused jealousy initially, as the school became more and more successful. Some also resented her education, as a woman, and someone who had lived abroad. But eventually she was accepted."

"So there have been no troubles around the school recently."

"No, no trouble." Lucy paused for a moment. No harm in telling this, she thought: "Someone wanted to buy the school property."

"Who is this?"

"I don't know the name. But he said that a company in Nairobi wants to build a brick factory. They want the playground and the neighbouring farm. But we can't have a school without the playground. It is a government requirement. So the parents' committee dismissed the offer like that," she said, snapping her fingers. "They want to buy a lot of land here. But we aren't going anywhere. No one is going to chase us away."

\*\*\*\*

## Aug. 2007

"T ELL ME A STORY about yourself that I can write in my book, Lucy," Kwamboka said to her friend. "I'll make it a book for secondary school students. There's nothing else like it. No book at all."

There were plans to expand the Malaika School to accommodate their graduates, as there was an acute shortage of secondary schools in the country. Kwamboka's American friend was raising funds and a survey had been conducted to determine whether the property next to the playground could be expanded to make room for a new building.

Lucy couldn't think of a story of her own worth repeating. Instead, she encouraged Kwamboka to talk to Dennis. This she did, before his neurological illness became debilitating.

"I don't have a story about me," Lucy continued to insist. No matter how vigorously Kwamboka disagreed, Lucy couldn't find an anecdote to relate.

"I do have a relative who has an interesting life. Would you like me to tell you about him?"

"Yes, please."

\*\*\*\*

*Moseti was my uncle, a brother to my mother. You could say that he was just a boy when he ran away from home to join the army, a few years after his initiation and shortly after my birth. He could hardly have been fifteen at the time. I don't think Moseti lied to the authorities about his age. He didn't have to say anything to justify his enlisting and they needed no convincing to take him. The British didn't question anyone who wanted to join the military ranks. The colonial government conscripted many men in Kenya and, as far as I could tell, rejected only those who were lame or blind. There was a great war going on and the British were happy to get one more body to save their empire. Most soldiers were sent out of the country, to Burma and other places in Asia, and most of them never made it back alive or if they did, they wished they had died in Burma instead. No one would speak about their time in the war. I think it may have been Moseti's youth that saved his life. He was slightly built and on the short side even as an adult. It was also near the end of the war when my uncle enlisted. Maybe there wasn't enough time to send him away. So he was stationed in Kenya throughout. He said he never fired a gun. He completed his entire army stint at a camp in the Rift Valley.*

*When the war ended, Moseti continued to live away from Kisii. The first time I can remember meeting him was when he came to visit my mother and I for a few days, when I must have been about five. I remember him visiting our home many times after that]; it seemed as though he came every year. On each visit he brought little packets of flower seeds that we planted by the front of the house. None of our neighbours had such a flower garden. It made me wonder about what other possibilities the world had waiting.*

*Moseti was bigger than life to me. He assumed the stature of a hero in my mind. He had been a soldier, after all. I knew no one else who worked so far away from Kisii or who knew Europeans the way he did. I remember he always drank his coffee without milk.*

*Moseti worked in many places around the country. By the time he was an old man, his services were greatly valued. I'm not sure where he is now. I haven't heard from him in quite a while. But I know this: he won't die rich, but he was pleased with how his life had unfolded.*

*He told many stories about himself. The one that most stays with me was the one about meeting an enemy officer. My uncle said that ever since then each time he digs in the damp soil on a cool morning and feels the black earth lodged under his fingernails and whenever he kneels over a flower bed to pull weeds and the sun beats on the folds in the back of his neck or any time the pungent aroma of marigolds wafts from the gardens he tends,  he remembers those days long before independence. And whenever he hears Italian tourists talking amongst themselves—"Ciao," "Bon giorno" and other phrases that are almost like his native tongue to him now— he is reminded of the Italian officer.*

*He remembers the first time he heard the Italian language being spoken at the prisoner of war camp for Italians that the British built near Gilgil, a camp known as Number 353.*

*Work for soldiers and prisoners was easy at this site, especially at the officers' quarters. Food was plentiful; the weather, while dry, was comfortably cool at nearly seven thousand feet above sea level. Because there wasn't much worry about escape, as it was difficult for an Italian to disappear into the vast expanse of plains or into the white settler town Nakuru by the flamingo lake, restrictions were minimal and security lax. The imprisoned officers even kept their own uniforms.*

*One day, Moseti stood behind the counter in the mess hall. He was dishing out a hot meal of ugali and tomato sauce on the officer's metal tray.*

*"Il mio amico," the officer said to Moseti. Moseti looked at the officer out of the corner of his eye. The person addressing him was about ten years older than himself and far better dressed. The Italian let out a hearty laugh. "This is a—what is the word?—a coincidence, I think you say. Here in British East Africa, I look at you and I find—what—a compatriot?" A soft voice issued from behind a thick, black moustache. "Did you steal your name?" the officer asked, obviously talking to Moseti, who was taken aback by being addressed by an Italian, by a prisoner.*

*Moseti raised his eyes from the steaming tray of food. He came to attention while the officer continued to speak to him. Moseti didn't know what to do. What was the officer saying? He, Moseti, thought that he was speaking English but was unsure with the accent being so odd. But it didn't sound like the language the POWs spoke amongst themselves, either. Moseti's English was passable. He understood the British soldiers when they spoke to one another as he had heard it often in Kisii at Gethin's garage and from the District Commissioner himself. He knew enough English to serve in the British military. But this was something new and unusual to him. Moseti looked blankly at the man in front of him, this prisoner with a clean and pressed uniform and straight hair made thick with pomade. He stood frightened, unable to speak.*

*The airman stared at Moseti's chest. "Moseti. Moseti. Moseti. That's an Italian name. Isn't it so? Like mine."*

*Still he didn't understand.*

*"Moseti. How did you ever get such a name? Is your family from Eritrea? Asmara is a beautiful city, like Italy, with cafes*

*and piazzas. Maybe my uncle had a family he didn't tell us about."* He laughed again.

Moseti didn't want to violate a regulation that would get him into trouble. He didn't know if it were permissible to talk to prisoners of war. Perhaps if he were a guard, he would know, but as someone who worked in the mess kitchen, he was ignorant. He was afraid that refusing to respond to an officer, even a prisoner, was a violation of the military code.

"Maybe you are Italian yourself. I am not from Sicily myself. But that uncle, maybe he stopped there, too. I know Sicilians almost as dark as you. Perhaps you baked in the sun a little too long, like bread kept too long in the oven." The officer laughed. Moseti didn't know what to do. "I long for a good loaf of bread. Just one loaf of bread and garlic," he continued as he moved his tray along. "In my country, this is called polenta. What do you call it?" he asked, pointing to the mound of cooked maize meal.

Was this officer serious? How was Moseti to answer; should he reply or pretend not to hear? The airman didn't wait for an answer from the African but put his cutlery on his tray and went to a bench to join his fellow officers.

The officer saw Moseti again later that week, outside the mess hall, as Moseti sat on his haunches next to the side of the building smoking a stub of a cigarette. The lieutenant, a muscular man with round dark eyes, walked up to Moseti. Moseti immediately stood at attention, his cigarette cupped in his hand.

"You're the one I saw the other day?" he queried. "The one with the stolen name." The officer walked closer to Moseti, who continued to stand motionless, afraid of doing the wrong thing. "How can I forget the African with the Italian name? It's a strange name for an African," the prisoner said, secure in his superior position. Moseti sensed a sincerity he had not experienced amongst the British soldiers. "But that makes a bond between us, two Italianos."

"Yes, afande," Moseti finally said. He was getting accustomed to the officer's accent and was beginning to understand the nature of the Italian's comments.

"Just look at this," the officer explained, as he pointed at his chest. "See here."

Moseti looked at the Italian's name.

"My name, your name, we are the same," the Italian said. "Lt. Modesti. And Pvt. Moseti. We are alike. One family."

"I am African. It's a name from my home, afande."

"What? Speak a little slower. My ears aren't as fast as my tongue. My spoken English is quite good, don't you think? I finished top in my class in college in Catania. I need practice. So slowly, please. What are you saying?"

"They call me Moseti, from my home, afande."

"Si. And my name is Modesti. Did I see you with a cigarette, amico? Do you have another cigarette for me? I left mine in the barracks." He gestured towards Modesti's hands, and then pointed to his mouth, pretending to blow smoke.

Moseti reached into his fatigue jacket and then held out his open hand to offer the few shreds of tobacco to the officer.

"Oh, no, no," he said, waving Moseti away. "No thanks. I'll get my own. Amico. Where are you from?" Before Moseti could answer, he asked, "Are you busy? Let's take a walk, back to my little hotel, for me to get my cigarette, if you don't mind."

How could Moseti refuse, how could he not accept an order from a superior, even if an enemy? He went with the POW, hoping no British soldier would see him.

"And where are you from?" the lieutenant asked again.

"Kisii."

"Where is that?"

My uncle was beginning to understand the officer. "Not far," he said.

*"You are from Kenya then?"*

*"Yes, afande," Moseti answered.*

*"Tell me about Kisii. Is that a village?" the airman wanted to know.*

*"Yes, afande, but not my village but my district. My farm," he continued but was interrupted by the Italian.*

*"Your farm? This is fantastico."*

*"Yes, my shamba," Modesti continued, "it is near Riosiri."*

*"Rio Siri? This is magnifico! The River Siri. Does Siri have a meaning?"*

*"In Swahili, not my language, afande."*

*"What does it mean in Swahili? Do you know?"*

*"Yes, sir. It means 'secret.' "*

*"You live by the Secret River. Why is the river a secret?"*

*"I don't know, sir."*

*"Maybe it is a secret from you, too."*

*"There is no secret, sir. There is no river."*

*"Rio but no river? No. It must be the war. In war everything is a secret."*

Only later did Moseti and Modesti clear up the muddle, sorting out the English, Swahili and Italian words. By then Moseti, too, heard the similarities that the airman had pointed to. Motari and Sagini, too, were names that sounded as though they could have come from Italy, Kisii neighbours to Andrietti, Iorio and Calvino. He understood the real, if only temporary, connection between the lieutenant and himself.

*"Are you from Sicily?" Modesti asked, in what Moseti had come to recognize as teasing. "A shepherd from the hill country, maybe?"*

Whenever Moseti saw Modesti in the mess hall, the officer greeted him warmly; pleased in the little joke they had created.

"Moseti, mio paisano," Modesti said as the two of them sat by a whistling thorn, watching zebra and giraffe graze in the distance. "Do you love flowers?"

"Yes, sir, we have flowers at my home." He had no idea what the Italian meant by loving flowers. "Flowers grow in Kisii," Moseti answered.

"Please, no more 'sir.' We are paisano, countrymen. About the flowers" he continued. "You must have flowers growing at your home. Flowers grow everywhere. Even in the desert, I've seen it myself, in North Africa. And here, even here there are wild flowers in our resort, even this dusty spa." He saw the puzzled look on Moseti's face. "This hotel of ours. This prison camp. Number 353." The corners of Moseti's mouth turned up. "So in this home of yours, yes, there must be flowers. But what kind?"

"Just flowers."

"Just flowers?"

"Just flowers. We wear them for ceremonies. When someone dies, we use flowers."

"We have flowers for funerals, too. But what kind of flowers are they?"

"Just flowers."

"Flowers aren't just flowers," Modesti said, the impatient teacher. "Are people 'just people'? No. Flowers are different, flowers are, what shall I say, like love."

"Flowers are just flowers."

"Flowers and love, they go together, of course."

"We have big flowers . . ."

"What colour?"

"The colour of lemons."

"Si."

"These are the ones we wear—big flowers—when someone dies. We put them on our bodies."

*ers to the women I love," Modesti said. "Roses,* *carnations. It doesn't matter. I buy them at the* *n the market, but mostly I like to bring to the* *nes I grow myself. You said you have a farm, didn't you? Every African has a farm, am I right?"*

*"In Kisii, we all have farms. Mine is on the other side of this valley, over there, where the sun sets. Where we have rain every day."*

*Lt. Modesti opened a pack of cigarettes and gave one to Moseti.*

*"And what flowers do you grow there in your garden?"*

*"I have cows on my shamba. Flowers are there." Moseti put the cigarette in his mouth; the airman lit it for him. "I don't plant them."*

*"You have a home with no flower garden?" the Italian said incredulously. "This is something amazing you are telling me."*

*"What good are flowers to plant? They are a hedge, that's all. On the farm we grow what we can eat. Bananas we can eat. They are like sugar."*

*"And flowers are like sunshine. Don't you hunger for beauty?"*

*"I look around my farm and I see green hills as far as I can see," my uncle said as he looked at the sere plains around him. "I see maize growing and I make a little money. 'Nzuri sana.' This is very good. I can't eat the sun. I look at my cows. The cows are beautiful and I get milk. So why do you plant flowers instead of having land for your cows or food?"*

*"This is my siri," the lieutenant commented wistfully. "I miss my flowers and my love."*

*"Someday we will both go home," Moseti said. "I want to eat my wimbi. It's time for me to become a wealthy man."*

*"Listen, my friend," Modesti said in a hushed voice, as he accosted Moseti on the walk between the barracks and the mess hall. "I arranged to have these sent to me." He opened*

his hand and showed Moseti a paper packet with a p
of yellow flowers. "We are going to plant these. Behind
barracks there is a patch of land. I can take water from the
pump."

Moseti looked at Modesti without saying a word. He waited
for the lieutenant to continue.

"The two of us, we are going to grow these flowers. I'll
show you how to make this hotel a beautiful place. These
flowers," Lt. Modesti explained, "are my favourite flowers of
all. They weren't easy to get. I had to give something big for
them. There is no smoke for us today. I had to use two packs
of cigarettes to get them."

"You used your cigarettes as bakshish?" Moseti asked.
"For flowers?"

"Si, of course. For these flowers I would do almost anything,"
Modesti answered. "But let me tell you, many people don't
like these, they don't like the smell. They say they stink. But
not to me. They smell like the earth. I grow only these by
the front door of my home. "There are other flowers I grow,"
he continued. He rubbed his finger along his moustache.
"But these, I also put them in the field, by the tomato plants.
The same smell that others hate, I love because they keep
the bugs away. Then I have my beautiful flowers and my
tomatoes."

Modesti sat on his haunches. Moseti did the same.

"Have you seen these before? Do you know what they are
named?"

"What do you mean, named?"

"The name."

"You name flowers, like children?"

"Not like children. Not like Pvt. Moseti or Lt. Modesti," he
smiled. "But the type of flower, the kind, the family."

Moseti looked at the package of seeds.

*"We have flowers that look like this. Maybe the mganga who uses flowers to heal the sick knows. Not me."*

*"They are Tagetes erecta, paisano. In Latin,"* the airman explained. *"In English, 'marigold.' The flower comes in two varieties, the dwarf, which is the French kind, and the giant, which is the African. I grow only the African."*

*"You don't like the French."*

*"Not because they are our enemy now. The French type is too precise. The African is more wild."* Moseti listened carefully. The Italian continued, *"Do you know why it is called Tagetes?"*

*"No."*

*"After a minor god from ancient Italy called Tages,"* Modesti said.

*"Your old God is a miner? What does he dig?"*

*"He didn't dig for anything."*

*"Then why was he a miner?"* Moseti didn't understand.

*"Oh, I see,"* the lieutenant answered with much sincerity. *"I mean that he was a small god. One god, Jupiter, was the general; others were colonels, majors and captains. Tages was like a lieutenant."*

*"What does this lieutenant god have to do with flowers?"*

*"That's what I'm going to tell you,"* Modesti said. *"The flower is beautiful like him. The story is that one day a farmer was in the field."*

Moseti interrupted Modesti.

*"What did the farmer grow?"*

*"I don't know. Let's say tomatoes."*

*"Tomatoes. They are good. I have tasted tomatoes. But were there any bananas?"*

*"No. I don't think so. We can't grow bananas in Italy and this is a story about a farmer who lived in Italy. Well, the story is that the farmer's plough left a furrow in the field and*

55

someone came out of the ground. This was Tages. Although he was only a boy, Tages had white hair like an old man. He was also wise like an old person."

Moseti listened intently.

"Tages is remembered for two things," Modesti continued.

"Yes?"

"First, he could predict the future by watching lightning. He went to the seven princes in the ancient kingdom and became their diviner."

"Yes. I also go to a diviner."

"Well, this diviner wrote his predictions in a book."

"Kisii diviners talk to you, they don't write."

"I understand," Modesti said.

"Tell me," Moseti insisted. "What did she say?"

"The diviner was a man." Modesti continued, "That's a good question you ask, but there is no answer. No one knows. Who can tell the future, anyway? The book is lost."

"In Kisii," Moseti began, "there was a prophet. His name was Sakawa. He also predicted the future. He didn't write a book, but people remember what he said."

"And what was that?"

"That someday people the colour of infants would come and they would rule us."

"He was right, your prophet. The English are like children."

"Yes," Moseti said. "The English came. They are pale like infants, not like you. So the first part was true."

"And the second part? What is that?"

"The second part is still coming true."

"And that is?"

"Someday they will leave."

"Yes, I hope so. No. I'm sure. They will leave."

They sat facing each other in silence. Finally Moseti said,

*"Then why do you remember Tages, if you don't know anything he said?"*

*«For the second thing, the thing that he is remembered for most. Not the prophecy."*

*"Yes?" Moseti wanted to know. "What is that?"*

*"His unusual beauty,» Modesti said. "What was so unusual about Tages is that he looked both young and old at the same time. He was born out of the earth, not from a mother but straight from the ground. He was beautiful because he was young. But he was also wise because he was old. That's why the flower is named after him."*

*"Why?"*

*"The flower is wonderful, like Tages, beautiful and wise, very unusual together," Modesti said, his hands circling in front of him. «The flower itself is also hope. To look at the golden colour is to make you feel the sun on your skin. They can be grown almost anywhere. In the sun they grow full. I have marigolds three feet tall at my home, up to here," he said, patting his thigh as he stood up. "In less sun the flower grows tamer and the foliage becomes denser and greener."*

*Modesti described the differences in the flowers at the seashore and on windy hillsides, how they survive in almost any soil and how, when other plants fail, marigolds succeed. "They look like royalty," he said, "but in their hearts they are democrats, they can't be killed, even by clumsy hands."*

*Moseti stood, too.*

*"Now, let's plant," Modesti said.*

*The two of them began to prepare the soil between the wooden building and the grove of acacia trees. They broke the soil with Moseti's trench tool, furrowed the ground with their fingers and planted the seeds in the thin soil. They sowed the seeds a quarter inch deep and a half inch apart, covered them with the loose soil, then pressed down firmly with their hands.*

When they finished, they stood next to each other.

"Look over there," Modesti said. A giraffe loped across the grassy field. Moseti watched. "Almost like a walking marigold."

"Beautiful," Moseti said.

The Italian officer found an old cloth in the barracks and covered the seedbed with it, keeping the soil damp. Four days later the two of them took the tarp off; tiny shoots sprouted from the ground. Several weeks later, Moseti saw the vivid yellow flowers for the first time and soon began to smell their peculiar odour.

The two of them lavished attention on their small garden, the profusion of flowers serving as a constant source of bouquets for the officers' mess hall. Modesti found much pleasure in growing marigolds and often wore one on the lapel of his only civilian shirt.

"You know the little church being built on the cliff?" Modesti asked Moseti.

"Yes," Moseti answered. Since the prisoners had arrived at the detention camp, they had been detailed to build the highway from Nairobi across the Rift Valley to the settler farmers on the western escarpment. When they completed the road, they had constructed a miniature chapel in commemoration of this feat.

"Have you seen it?"

"No. I never go that way on the road. My home is the other direction. I've never been to Nairobi."

"Then I think we should go for a visit," Modesti said. "I want to see it before I leave."

"We can't go."

"Yes we can. All we need to do is walk out the front gate."

The war in Europe was over. The prisoners were being repatriated. Why would anyone care that they left for a day to visit a holy shrine?

Moseti arranged for the two of them to get a hitch in one of the jeeps. No one asked for their passes. They rode through the gate and down the road. When they returned, Moseti was put in the brig.

No visitors were allowed to visit the African prisoners. On the first day, he received a dozen marigolds. But he didn't hear from Modesti after that. When Moseti was released from the prison, he discovered that Modesti had been shipped out with fifty other Italians.

Moseti didn't return to Kisii after the war. He first found employment in Nairobi working at a flower nursery, then for the city council tending the plants and trees in the avenue divides. In time he found work as a groundskeeper at a ranch belonging to a white settler, near Nyeri, in Central Province. That farm became part of one of the settlement schemes and my uncle never had a chance to purchase land there since he wasn't a Kikuyu and didn't know anyone in high office. So after uhuru, he found employment as the chief grounds keeper and manager at Swift Water Safari Club. That's where I last saw Uncle Moseti. Once I went with Kombo on one of his work drives that took him to that part of the country and my uncle and I talked for hours one night at his two room concrete house near the riverbed. Many books on horticulture were neatly piled in stacks as tall as he. He looked just as I had remembered him—robust, with strong hands deeply stained with soil, supremely happy in his work. Moseti never married and had been living at the club for many years, the dwelling fit for a man of some consideration.

"I am treated well," he says. "I am respected by everyone."

In the shadow of the snowy peaks of Mt. Kenya, he kept the grass on the golf course sparkling green and grew lilies and roses, passion flowers and birds of paradise, trumpet vine, sweet smelling gardenias and jasmine and frangipani. He tended succulents and cactus, blossoms and flowering trees, some plants indigenous to the equatorial highlands, *some never seen before in East Africa. My uncle knew them all by their common and Latin names. And of course he grew marigolds, the African kind.*

*I asked him about the Italian soldier with the Kisii-sounding name. He said that he never heard from him after the war. He once inquired after him at the Italian Embassy in Nairobi. He wanted to know how he might find the repatriated airman, but the task seemed insurmountable. He even once wrote to the mayor of Catania, hoping the letter would reach Modesti. The letter wasn't returned and there was no reply, either.*

*On those days when my uncle prepared the soil, carefully, gently with a trowel, then scratched the ground and sniffed the deep aroma of soil and heard the one foreign language that reminded him of our mother tongue, he looked up to glance at the tourists from Rome or Milan or Florence, talking, drinking coffee, and laughing with one another.*

*"I almost ask if they know Lt. Modesti from Catania," he said to me.*

*But he didn't ask and instead hoped that someone would approach him when they read the name that is sewed above the left breast pocket of his green cotton shirt, and he would say, "Yes, that's my name," and he would introduce himself—"Mi chiamo Tages Moseti"—and at first the Italian visitors would be puzzled, but then they would understand why he called himself by such a name the moment he handed them a bouquet of orange flowers for their dining table.*

*As far as I know, no one ever asked.*

# Rivers of Beer

PLASTIC CHAIRS that have been rented for the funeral service arrive and are arranged in rows on the lawn in front of the church. Red moulded chairs with Coca-Cola logos stamped on them, which have been borrowed from several Kabungu cafés and hotels, are scattered about. Those seated on the grass find a newly arrived chair and turn the seat to face the person they are conversing with. A few continue to squat on low wooden stools that they have brought themselves.

Kwamboka's funeral serves as a kind of reunion for parents of children who have graduated from the Malaika School but no longer live in Kisii and for former students who have moved away, to Eldoret, Nairobi, Mombasa or perhaps even Uganda or Tanzania. One graduate now works with refugees from Sudan in a camp in the northern desert, several are teachers themselves, one is a nurse, another just returned from Canada with her journalism degree. Gladys Nyagaka is a doctor at the Kabungu Health Centre; she graduated from Abilene Christian University Medical School, in Texas. Queenie Masanja is a music teacher at the Music School of Eastern Africa. Nancy Nyaboke is a free-lance journalist.

Dingiria notices young women line up to greet Rebecca Nyanchoka. The inspector moves closer to listen. He surmises these are former students from the Malaika School. He hears the retired teacher ask about each of her former students.

Pupils from other area schools are seated on the grass. The current Malaika students are beyond the fence, on the slope by the tea field. The awnings of the smaller tents shelter former students and friends of Kwamboka. The rest of the assembly stands in the heat, the mid-day sun. Birds are resting, except for vultures that continue to circle high over the small slaughterhouse that is on the other side of the hill behind the church.

Ranking police officers stride in from the road, one in a blue uniform, another in a khaki uniform. Both are bedecked with ribbons and the one in khaki carries a baton. Two policemen in khakis and berets accompany them. Men in suits shake hands with the officers as they are escorted to the white tent. Enlisted police stand near the cypress fence. Dingiria stands near at the far end of one of the smaller shelters. He wonders how the guests will receive the information he plans to deliver. He knows what he wants to say, but isn't certain of the wording. He needs to be precise. He worked on his comments for hours the day before. Even as the funeral has progressed, he has made additional notes and scratched out some previous remarks. His training has taught him how to remain calm, but this time his palms begin to sweat. He hasn't felt like this since the first day he was accepted into the force. Dingiria knows that after he talks to the gathered there is no turning back. He worries that he will not be able to control his voice. Should he consult his notes? He should be precise but it would distance him from the group and he would lose his nerve if he didn't speak directly.

Not as elaborate as Luo funerals, which Dingiria has read can and sometimes do pauperize a family, in Kisii when someone of Kwamboka's stature dies, especially under horrific circumstances, everyone makes an effort to attend the service, coming from all corners of the country. When there are relatives who live abroad, a body may be kept refrigerated for several weeks until they are able to attend. But Kwamboka has no family. Lucy had hoped that Kwamboka's American friend, the school's benefactor, would attend, but it took several days to contact her; by then the date for the service had been set and there wasn't enough time for Lena Morrell to get to Kisii for the service.

He decided to wear his police uniform to the funeral. He never liked wearing the stiff police outfit; he preferred not calling attention to himself. This was one reason why he preferred being a detective. Another is that the work was much like the jigsaw puzzles that he enjoyed putting together. But for this occasion, since this was a public forum he thought that donning his uniform was the best way to make it clear that he represented the national police. That way, there would be no misunderstanding as to who he is, no misrepresentation.

Dingiria watches Lucy shake hands with men and women as they arrive on the compound. She escorts them either to the table or the tent. She hands them a printed program and points to the paper she has on a clipboard to show them where they fit in the schedule. Discussions ensue; Lucy takes a pen and makes some notes. Some aren't pleased with her decision, but she is firm.

The sky is clear and the colour of pale lavender. It hasn't rained for several weeks, an unusual occurrence where afternoon downpours are typical. Other parts of the country are experiencing drought. No one expects that here, but the lack of afternoon rain is worrying. Some crops are beginning to wilt. Yesterday the sky darkened at about 4.00 P.M. There was a rumble of thunder, but it was only a tease. A few drops fell, hardly enough to raise the drooping heads of thirsting plants.

****

## 20 Feb. 2009

WHEN DINGIRIA WENT TO INTERROGATE the young men, they had already been arraigned and remanded. A trial would quickly follow.

The inspector approved of such swift action. 'Justice delayed is justice denied.' This was one of the lessons he took from reading Beccaria at the police college. It was because the Italian reformer also argued that education was one of the keys to preventing crime that Dingiria felt so repulsed by the murder of an educator.

Confessions from the young men were in hand. The day following the night-time murder, before Dingiria was assigned the investigation from the provincial headquarters, a KTN reporter had said that the men had told the police that the killing was just a day's work. The TV report was mainly a reading of the press release issued by the police; the same with the second page article in two major newspapers that appeared the next day. There was no independent reporting on the case and, if another article appeared at all, it would indicate that the young men had been sentenced.

While the killers were locked away, what remained unknown was the motive behind the crime; the accused said nothing about who had employed them. Their involvement was strictly business.

The three murderers were held in one tight cell without windows. There was one bed and no toilet. After peering at the men through bars of their cell, Dingiria went to the interrogation room. Before questioning the first man, Dingiria turned on the overhead light, took out a pad and pen and placed them on the table. A police officer opened the door to the room and the first man entered, unshackled. He was wearing an American baseball cap with the letters UM, an orange polo shirt, brown pants and sneakers. The others were similarly dressed, that is, much like jobless men their age, their clothes bought from the racks of second-hand goods' sellers at an outdoor market.

When he was done with the three, he reviewed the interrogations, such as they were. Dingiria had noticed bloodstains mixed with mud on the running shoes of one and on the sleeve of the T-shirt shirt of another. While their clothes were shabby, none were dishevelled. They appeared tired but not abused. The detective made a mental note of this. It was odd, he thought, that they had no bruises, no signs of being roughed up by the police: just a swollen lip and an eye closed shut, a cut on the forehead—minor things. Petty thieves received worse treatment. Perhaps he would have to do it himself, to get more information from them if they continued to be indifferent to his questions. His mentor, Beccaria, argued that severe punishment was needed as a deterrent. But the inspector would only go so far, stopping before torture. Dingiria saw officers cross that line, but he would never do that, although there were times when he had to restrain himself. The frustration he felt when confronted with a criminal's obduracy occasionally pushed him to the edge and he wondered if some of his methods were, in fact, torture. The Italian philosopher had persuaded him that torture had no place in an interrogator's arsenal. "By this method the robust will escape, and the feeble be condemned," was the line that he remembered from *On Crimes and Punishments*. He had to monitor himself closely in this situation.

Each of the accused had entered the room unencumbered by cuffs or leg irons. The guard, on his own initiative, left the room, closed the door behind him, leaving Dingiria alone with the killers.

The oldest was still in his teens, the other two still boys. Their eyes weren't hard or dead, unlike those of some soulless monsters he had dealt with. They showed no remorse, no shame or guilt. Instead, Dingiria sensed a hint of pride in those who sat in front of him. It was as though these were weary youths at the end of a long day, worn down by too much drinking. Inspector Dingiria asked them a few questions, but they gave no more information than what he already knew. There was nothing more he would get from them that day.

He returned to his temporary office at the Kabungu station and opened up the file folder containing Kwamboka's manuscript. He found a chapter with the following handwritten introduction:

*It is difficult to imagine what it was like at the time known as Uhuru, when we were finally rid of the British rule. There have been so many disappointments since those heady days. But anyone who came of age before 1964 remembers the time well. There hasn't been anything like it since, not even the first multi-party election or the voting for our first truly democratic president.*

*Maurice Osiemo lived through that time, just as I did. I didn't know him, but his sister, Rebecca, was a teacher at my school. She is a collector. In her house are soaps and matchboxes from hotels she has visited. There are many magazines on the floor. She also records important events in her life. One day she showed me a newspaper clipping that she keeps in her scrapbook. It is the front page of the Daily Nation when Kenyatta was sworn in, and there is a photo of the lowering of the Union Jack. We sat together drinking tea as we reminisced. She stopped when she got to a small clipping, something not more than fifth of the page.*

*"We didn't know at the time," she says, as she points to the yellow page. "And today, no one remembers. Do you?"*

Dingiria called Alfred Nyang'wara into his room, no bigger than the cell of the prisoners he had visited. He pointed to Kwamboka's comments appended to the story, "Rivers of Beer."

"You're from this area, aren't you?" he asked the clerk.

"I was born here, sir."

"Have you lived anywhere else?"

"I've only worked in Kisii," he answered.

"Do you know someone named Osiemo?" Dingiria asked the clerk.

"There are a few by that name."

"Maurice Osiemo."

The clerk sat for a minute. The only sound was the cawing of crows high in the tree outside the police building. He had little desire to co-operate with the visiting policeman.

"No."

"A brother of someone named Rebecca Nyanchoka. A teacher at the Malaika School."

"I don't know him," the clerk said, trying to hide his impatience.

"And Nyanchoka?"

Nyang'wara shrugged his shoulders.

"Maybe a new teacher. Or an old one. I don't know everyone who teaches there."

Dingiria asked Nyang'wara to bring him a pot of coffee. The clerk took a minute before he rose from his chair to comply.

****

THAT DAY DINGIRIA READ Rebecca Nyanchoka's story about her brother. He then sought her out for an interview, to see if there was something more to the story, a clue cleverly hidden by Kwamboka.

Dingiria discovered Nyanchoka living on the other side of Kisii, near the stone quarries. Her home was down a steep incline off the road. She had one coffee tree, long neglected, and two banana plants by her front door. A chicken clucked as it scrambled across the grass and ducked into a hedge. Millet and onions grew in the plot next to the house.

Nyanchoka lived in a two-room mud house with a metal roof. Behind the house was a cooking room and a little further downhill, a latrine. This was her late husband's home. Rebecca Nyanchoka's four sons, with their wives and children, lived in the surrounding compounds.

When the inspector drove his government-issued Peugeot on the property, a wiry dog ran up to the inspector. As was his habit when visiting rural homes during the day, Dingiria put his pistol in the car's glove compartment, then made sure the doors to the car were also locked when he stepped out. The dog first snarled, then barked at his heels. A boy wearing short pants and a clean worn-out T-shirt squeezed through the hedge separating Rebecca's house from the next. The dog calmed down in the boy's presence. Dingiria asked if this was the home of Mama Nyanchoka. Seeing the badge the inspector produced, the boy began to tremble.

"No problem, *kijana*," he assured him. "I just want to ask her a few questions."

An old woman, stooped and using a staff to walk, greeted Dingiria in English. Initially surprised, he chided himself. Many of her age mates wouldn't know English. But she was a teacher, after all—in one of the best primary schools around Kabungu. He sat with her for a while. Her comments confirmed what he already heard: Kwamboka had withdrawn from school activities and returned to more scholarly pursuits, enjoying her retirement from public scrutiny and coaxing stories from those she knew.

****

*The story begins early in 1965, when Maurice Osiemo walked several miles down the dirt road from our small farm at the top of Manga escarpment, crossed the bridge over the surging river by the factory of the coffee co-operative and strode into town. His brow was wet with sweat, his feet aching and hot in the black gum boots, his heart jumping with anticipation. He sat by the Post Office for a few minutes, watched someone remove a letter from a post box, then turned his attention to the street where he enjoyed the sight of women walking to the market, their goods piled high on their heads. Across the road was the prison; he was certain soon all the prisoners would be released, free to live their lives as Kenyan citizens, no longer held behind wire fences, made to chop wood.*

*Maurice bought a paper cone of groundnuts from a young boy for ten cents, stood in front of the farm supply store next to bags of fertilizer and seed until he finished the nuts, then continued further into town. He watched a man sitting on a stool behind a glass case on the sidewalk. 'Fundi Wa*

*Saa.' Maurice marvelled at the number of watches that the repairman had sprawled before him. He was certain that some were gold, left behind by one of the wazungu who couldn't wait to leave.*

*Next he stopped beside the tailor who pumped the treadle of the sewing machine, gliding the needle through cloth, repairing a pair of trousers. Maurice walked further down the hill, looking in the windows of the many shops along the main street, imagining himself in that new shirt, wearing a pair of socks, using a bright torch to illuminate his way home at night. He studied the picture of a European wearing a suit that was said never to wrinkle. Maurice could see himself walking into the Indian provisions shop one day and buying whatever it was that the wazungu's bought there. His pockets would be brimming with all sorts of modern, wondrous things.*

*In those days, soon after uhuru, there was a glow upon the earth. The symbols of change were everywhere. The new republican flag snapped in the wind on the knoll in front of the District Commissioners headquarters, its shield and spears guardians of this once-again black man's land. Her Highness had disappeared from the walls of the former colony, the photographs in every office and shop replaced with that of His Excellency Jomo Kenyatta, the erstwhile detainee and present president, his one hand grasping a silver-tipped sceptre and the other a fly whisk, his face determined and kind. When he saved enough money, Maurice would buy a photo of Mzee Kenyatta and put it on the wall of his own house, the new one he would build. He would be a wealthy man without as much as a callous on his hands or corns on his feet. Next to Mzee's photo would be one that he and his family would sit for at the photographer's shop in town.*

*The Queen wasn't the only missing person, Maurice noted as he walked down the town's paved road. The complexion of the town had turned decidedly darker. The remaining wazungu's were mainly missionaries and the few expatriates were from places he had never heard of, obscure bits on the European map. Only one British civil servant remained, the odd one who could speak Gusii. It was rumoured that an American family lived in town and had two large white cars.*

*Maurice crossed the Sports Club golf course—once an exclusive preserve for the white government officers—and through the fence by the building, he saw wahindi wearing short white trousers and white shirts hitting balls over nets. The Indians had inherited the game from the departing wazungu's, a sport Maurice didn't understand but found amusing to watch. An old man wearing a castoff military overcoat sat on his haunches near three zebu cows by the fourth hole. Maurice couldn't believe how brazen Africans had become, bold in a way he never thought possible, an omogaka fearing no white, trespassing with impunity.*

*Maurice doubled back into town, then walked downhill again to the west end, stopping by a garage on the upper road to chat with a friend. The two listened to a phonograph playing a song with a jaunty beat and indecipherable lyrics.*

*"The song is from Kisumu," Jonah said. Jonah was covered with grease from the car that lay a hundred pieces in front of him. "It's the Siaya Boys. How do you like it, Maurice?"*

*"I don't understand Luo. What are they singing about? I don't know, do you? Give me Malaika," he said. "I can sing that to my girl."*

*Maurice sang the plaintive lyric about not having enough money to marry. "Those black necks talk nonsense. What can I do with this music?"*

*"Dance," Jonah answered quickly. He grabbed a tool, wrapped his hand around it and shook it in front of Maurice. "That's what you can do. Like this," he said, as though dancing with the spanner. "The Twisti." He ground his heels into the deeply stained dirt.*

*Maurice laughed, too.*

"What are you doing later?" Jonah asked his friend.

"Nothing. I'm going back home." Maurice sat on a pile of worn tires while Jonah turned his attention to the axle in front of him. A large tree cast its shade over them both.

"There's a movie tonight at the cinema," Jonah said. "Stay with me. Go home tomorrow."

Why not? Maurice enjoyed spending the night in town and sleeping on a mattress, even if it meant sharing it with his friend.

"I'll meet you at the cinema when I'm finished," Jonah explained as he returned to his work.

It was still mid-afternoon. So Maurice walked back to the main road, crossed the paved avenue, examined the cardboard displays through the window of the photographer's shop, then, at the Hangover Butchery and Bar, sat at a large table occupied by a few other men. He grasped the metal cup of steaming tea. He ordered a crispy, meat-filled 'samosa' from the Somali owner. Maurice didn't know any of the other men in the restaurant.

The customer on the bench next to Maurice turned to him. After a formal greeting in Swahili, the stranger introduced himself. "Jina langu Wilson," he said. "Jina lako nani?"

"Maurice."

They chatted. Wilson asked Maurice what he was doing in town. The man was neatly dressed in a shirt like the type Maurice had admired earlier at the Popover Fashion Centre. Although Maurice wasn't accustomed to talking to someone he didn't know, this was time for uhuru. That, Maurice believed, meant talking to all Kenyans as though they were friends already.

"I am just walking about," Maurice responded. He noticed Wilson's sunglasses in his pocket shirt and the wristwatch peeking out from under the shirt cuff of his left sleeve. "Nothing special today. I want to look."

"This is the first time I am in Kisii," Wilson said. "Is there some place good for me to stay?"

Maurice had never stayed anywhere but with Jonah at his flat.

"There is a hotel on the street between here and the Indian *dukas* on the top of the hill," Maurice said, surprising himself with his authoritative tone. He turned in his seat and pointed the way with his lifted chin. Maurice admired Wilson's appearance—the neatly cropped hair, the leather shoes, the nylon tie. He looked like the man in the mosquito coil repellent advertisements.

"Don't you drink beer?" Wilson asked.

"I drink," Maurice said. In fact, he didn't have money for a Pilsner.

"Then let me buy you a beer."

Maurice agreed. The day was turning out as good as he had hoped. Here was proof that *uhuru* meant beer flowing like rivers, just as the Bible promised. Maurice shared his 'samosa.' Wilson ordered more.

Maurice told Wilson that he owned a farm at the top of the rocky escarpment several miles from Getembe—"That is what we Kisii's call this town."

Wilson inquired after his children.

"A man your age should be married."

Maurice described his plight.

"Then this is your lucky day," Wilson said. He finished his pint of beer and ordered another for himself and Maurice. "I am the man for you. This is why I am here, to find a smart man who wants to become wealthy."

Wilson gave an account of himself as an agent for a big company—a firm with connections in State House, White House, 10 Downing Streets and other impressive-sounding places. He was looking for men such as Maurice. Whatever question Maurice had about the nature of the work, Wilson *deflected with more copious descriptions of the success that awaited Maurice by year's end.*

*"Oh, yes," he said. "This is your day, Maurice."*

*If Maurice would meet him at the hotel after the movie, Wilson would tell him more about the fortune waiting to be taken. Dark clouds bulked above the hills and the rumble of thunder rolled across the valley. Jonah would be finished with work soon.*

*Maurice finished another beer, thanked Wilson and left the bar. Feeling buoyant, he stopped at the stationers to buy a chocolate bar, a treat that he had only heard about before. Maurice then walked to the cinema. He looked at the poster announcing the movie for the night. Once inside, Maurice would find out why young people in America sat on sand wearing only their underwear. Now he would have the opportunity to see America as it really was.*

*Maurice and Jonah sat next to each other on wooden crates. After the cinema darkened, a song, which Maurice had heard only once before at the Independence Day celebrations at the municipal stadium, played while the national flag was shown on the screen. This was followed by the American movie. Maurice could have watched the movie a second time. He enjoyed looking at the nearly naked wazungu on the beach, in their cars without tops, in the most beautiful houses he had ever seen. Jonah said he didn,t like the show. He was too embarrassed seeing people in their undergarments.*

*Maurice told his friend that he wanted to meet the man he had talked to earlier at the bar. He invited Jonah to join him. When they entered the hotel, Maurice saw Wilson on a stool next to the bar. A half-empty bottle of Pilsner stood in front of him.*

*"You,ve invited a friend, too," Wilson said, this time less polite than in the afternoon. He seemed irritated, as though Maurice were bothering him. «That,s good. Maybe he wants a job, too.»*

"I have a good job," Jonah explained. He told him he was a mechanic at a garage.

"You're working for an Asian?" Wilson said off-handedly. "This isn't why we have uhuru. Do you call that freedom? Work for a black man."

Jonah had heard about mechanics in other parts of the country who were talking about action against Indian garage owners. Perhaps Wilson was a trade union organizer. Did he know Tom Mboya, the big man from Rusinga?

"I am offering you exciting work," he continued, "where you become wealthy in a short time and have enough money to buy more land and have several wives."

Maurice pictured the silk dresses and silver spangles, the blue and white cars larger than any in Kenya, on roads wider than any highway in Africa.

"And what is this work?" Jonah inquired sceptically.

"I can't tell you that," Wilson said as he looked at his watch. "I can't reveal secrets like that. This is for those who have courage. It is for men who want to breathe the new air of 'uhuru.' I like Maurice. He looks to me like a hard-working man. If he wants the job, I am offering it to him now. And if you want to come, too, I think I can arrange that."

"What do I have to do?" Maurice asked eagerly.

"You will find out when you get there."

"Where do I have to go?"

"Then you want the job?"

Maurice looked at his friend. Jonah took his hand.

"Look at your friend here," Wilson said with scorn. "His clothes are full of grease. His hands aren't the hands of an educated man. And how much money does he make? Does he own a watch? Does he have a new shirt?" Before Jonah could respond, Wilson continued. "Look at me. Your friend fixes cars. I drive them. I'm a big man. You can be a big man, too. If you want your chance, tonight is the night."

*"Tonight?"*

*"Yes," Wilson said. "I'm leaving tonight. I'm inviting you to become rich. But you have to decide tonight."*

*Maurice began to protest.*

*"The choice is yours, mwananchi." Wilson emptied his bottle of beer. "I'm leaving now. Come with me, if you like, or remain a poor man all your life."*

*Maurice turned to Jonah for advice.*

*"Why ask him?" Wilson said. "Do you want to spend your life covered in grease, too?"*

*Maurice thought that Wilson was lucky that Jonah didn't have a screwdriver in his pocket; he knew that Jonah would have driven it into this man's heart.*

*"I think you should come home with me tonight," Jonah said. "You can think about it tomorrow."*

*"There is no tomorrow," Wilson said. "I'm leaving now. Come if you want. It makes no difference to me. I am making an offer. You can come with me or stay here and marry a lame old woman."*

*Wilson rose from the stool, walked to the door and left. "I'm going," Maurice said. "I'm going with him now."*

*"Don't be a fool."*

*Maurice ran after Wilson.*

*"I'm going with you!"*

*He could see Wilson's white teeth in the dark.*

*"Follow me," he said. Jonah stood at the doorway as the two of them walked to the upper road and then down a lane near the hospital. A flat-back truck waited there, the back filled with a dozen men, boys really, some as young as ten. Maurice was the oldest person there.*

*Wilson climbed into the cab, the engine turned over, the headlights were turned on and the gears ground as the truck disappeared into the dark.*

"No one heard from Maurice," Rebecca said. "It was as though he had been swallowed by the earth. Jonah wondered and waited for a letter, eager for some news, but none was forthcoming. My family, too, had no idea what had happened to him."

More than a year passed.

On March 19, 1966, the Daily Nation published the following article:

**Perhaps as many as 100 youths, age 11-15 have been taken by racketeers and forced to work as virtual slave labourers in sawmills on farms in the Moshi area.**

The article also noted that many of the youths kidnapped and taken to Moshi were Kisii's and, now that the illegal human-smuggling ring had been uncovered, many were to be repatriated.

Government messengers informed families that their sons were arriving in Kisii on Sunday morning. Several families and friends gathered silently by the district court. The usual crowds found in the government quarter were absent. All the offices were closed. The only sounds were those of the raucous crows in the towering trees. By mid-afternoon, people were thirsty and hungry.

Rebecca sent word to Jonah that his friend was coming home. Jonah now waited with Maurice's relatives. Not one person spoke during those long hours.

Late that afternoon, a lorry stopped on the street in front of the Department of Co-operative Development. A policeman pulled up the canvas curtain on the back of the truck. The one-time recruits stood as quietly as cords of wood, their faces without expression, their eyes blank and far away.

One policeman lowered the tailgate of the lorry. "Haraka, haraka," another urged. "The trip is long enough. Hurry up. Step out! It's Sunday. We want to go home."

*One-by-one the dispirited young men climbed from the back of the truck. Maurice was one of the last to descend. He stood next to the lorry until Rebecca and her family walked over to him. His eyes were cast at the ground. Jonah wasn't sure if Maurice had seen him. He remained as silent as Maurice.*

*Rebecca took Maurice by the arm and walked to the road that led to Manga hill. Jonah returned to his flat. He needed to be at the garage by dawn. Sunday was meant to be a day of rest and restoration.*

*"I saw Jonah several times after that and he asked about Maurice," Rebecca said. She told him that Maurice didn't want to see anyone. He stayed indoors all day and barely talked to his family. Jonah wondered if he would ever see Maurice again.*

*"He tried, though," Rebecca said.*

*During the first year Jonah came to the house a few times, but Maurice acted as though Jonah was invisible. He ignored him completely. Maurice was like this with almost everyone. He said a few words to me, but when he came home he had become like an enfeebled old man. He died a few years later. He had never left the farm before his family buried him.*

# The Power Line
## 28 Feb. 2009
## 1 P.M

DOZENS OF GUESTS QUEUE up waiting to sign the ledger that is opened on a podium inside the large tent. Dingiria sees that Anna Okiamba is amongst them.

Lucy leaves the gathering in front of the African Independent Church of Christian Disciples. She is wearing a *busuti,* a floor length dress with puffed shoulders, short sleeves and a square neckline, a gift given to her by Dennis after one of his Uganda races. Zion, in a simple dress and a black headscarf, leaves with her. The two walk about a kilometre down the Gesima road and turn into a lane by the Malaika School for Little Angels, at Kwamboka's home, a garden of yellow flowers by the front door.

A hush descends on the church lawn as people realize that Lucy has gone to Kwamboka's home. Without a family, Lucy has taken charge of the funeral. She is treated like the closest bereaved relative. Condolences are first paid to her.

Earlier, the police barricaded the road between Kwamboka's house and the church to prevent traffic from interfering with the service. By now there is a considerable backup of vehicles at both blockades. The traffic police try to turn the vehicles around, but the road is narrow and vehicles are wedged tightly in all directions. Drivers ask for an explanation. None are going to leave their vehicles unattended, so they sit in their cabs and doze or wait by the roadside, lean against the doors of their vehicles, engage in small talk with strangers.

At the church compound, it is as though the air itself has gone to sleep. The silence  reminds the *wazee* what it sounded like before trucks, lorries, buses, cars, motorcycles, and *matatus* became routine even on tertiary roads—before the straining engines of large trucks hauling rocks and those filled with sacks of fresh tea just processed at the factory, horns, music from *matatus*, the barking of touts. This is the silence before Kabungu was found on road maps, before electricity, even before radios, the silence that not even the night-time today knows.

Those on the queue take their seats.

When the police realize that the conversation has ceased and a sombre tone has replaced the previous conviviality, they break their circle of chatting and face the road, their shoulders nearly touching. The police aren't there because they are anticipating trouble. The Chief wanted them there, along with other shows of government concern. Dingiria argued that it would be better if they remained on the road. The police were held in such low esteem that Dingiria thought it would be a provocation. However, this wasn't his decision to make.

There is a brief service at the house. Zion stands in a circle and says, "Lord, you have been our dwelling-placein all generations. Before the mountains were brought forth or ever you had formed the earth and the world, from everlasting to everlasting you are God. You turn us back to dust, and say, 'Turn back, you mortals.' For a thousand years in your sight are like yesterday when it is past, or like a watch in the night." She stops now and again throughout the recitation to translate from Gusii into English.

"You sweep them away; they are like a dream, like grass that is renewed in the morning; in the morning it flourishes and is renewed; in the evening it fades and withers."

Zion had asked Lucy if she could offer the prayer at the house. Lucy agreed but only if she chose the verse. Out of respect for Kwamboka's religious sensibilities, Lucy chooses a psalm from the Old Testament, thereby avoiding references to Jesus.

Zion couldn't understand Kwamboka's spiritual orientation, which seemed vague, and she strongly disagreed with her indifference to matters of salvation. Kwamboka said that she hoped to be judged by the work that she did. Zion thought Kwamboka was being stubborn. It must have been Kwamboka's time in America that had turned her to such foolishness. Americans think they can do anything, even enter the gates of heaven without receiving Jesus as their personal saviour. Zion urged Kwamboka to join Finlay Abuga's Sweet Chariot Resurrection Ministries. Kwamboka's fierce argument with Pastor Abuga foreclosed that possibility and led Zion back to the AICCD. She couldn't understand Kwamboka but her respect for her was as deep as anyone's.

Lucy stood beside Zion as she recited the 90th psalm in Gusii.

Zion concluded with the translation from the last verse: "Let the favour of the Lord our God be upon us, and prosper for us the work of our hands—O prosper the work of our hands."

"Amen."

****

### 23 Feb. 2009

ON DINGIRIA'S SECOND visit to the jail, it was clear to him that the accused didn't know who had ordered the murder. It was just as they had said, he believed: they were the triggermen, nothing more or less. Sungusungu had nothing to do with the crime. These were murderers for hire. The oldest of the three appeared to be the leader. The others had no information to give.

"Did you know Prof. Kwamboka?" the inspector asked.

None did. They had never heard of her.

"Then why her?" Dingiria asked.

The leader explained that he had received a telephone call and he agreed to bring along two friends to do the job.

"Who called?"

The teenager shrugged his shoulders. He didn't know his name.

"What did he ask you to do?"

"Kill the lady."

"Did he say why he wanted her dead?"

"No. I didn't ask."

The inspector wanted to know why they had been contacted.

The young man didn't ask that either. But thought it was probably because they were members of Sungusungu and that they would carry out the request.

"Did you get your money?"

The young men said that they wouldn't do the job without getting paid first. They were instructed to go to a shopping plaza on the main street in Kisii Town. Under the pad of computer #5 in the cyber café, they would find half the money, as an advance. They would collect the rest after they finished the job.

"Was the money there?"

"It was."

"How much?"

"Ten thousand shillings. For each of us. Thirty thousand, all together."

Dingiria was taken aback by the amount. This was a month's wage for a police officer. By the look of their shabby clothes, Dingiria estimated that this was probably more money than they saw in six months.

Dingiria found the men's story plausible. They were like other young men who had been paid a few dollars to a kill with poisoned arrows and hard wooden clubs and to burn down houses in mixed areas after the disputed election results in which both sides claimed fraud, intimidation and chicanery. At a pay rate exceeding the total yearly income of the average Kenyan, it didn't matter whether the victims were strangers or enemies, or long-time neighbours or school chums. Several died in this region and hundreds of families were displaced.

Dingiria understood how desperation leads to corruption. He had seen much of it in the police force and he wasn't going to judge his fellow officers. His concern was only with major crimes. Bribes were just another form of business. It was a prominent Kisii politician, after all, who had said that police officers were paid so poorly that they couldn't afford underpants for their wives. The president himself said that the cars the police were driving were so old that they couldn't even chase a goat. He knew the joke that the police officer's way of saying hello is "Kitu kidogo," a little something.

"Did you collect the rest of the money?" the detective inquired.

They found the money as instructed. They thought maybe they would just take the first payment and head to Nairobi. Even half the amount was plenty.

"But you didn't," Dingiria said.

No, they wanted the entire amount. They didn't know when they would have so much again. So they took pangas and a pistol and broke into the house.

"Why didn't you take anything?"

This was an assassination, not a robbery.

"We were told to make it look like Sungusungu."

"You are Sungusungu," the inspector said.

"Not for this. It was supposed to look like Sungusungu. But this wasn't Sungusungu. They wanted us because we aren't afraid to kill."

The men said that the night after the murder the police arrested them as they were eating roast meat and getting drunk and flashing around some money at a hotel in Ikonge.

"We are Sungusungu. We didn't think we would be arrested. We have worked with the police before. We went in their vans to break up ODM protesters before the election."

"Maybe the police didn't know who you were."

The youth looked at Dingiria and said nothing.

Some in the community had used Sungusungu to kill witches. Witches were so dangerous that they had to be gotten rid of; they killed innocent people out of jealousy. People believed that they were employed to cause children to do poorly in school. Perhaps someone thought that Kwamboka had used a curse so that children in schools other than the Malaika School would fail. But this wasn't the way witches were murdered. There was no chopping of the body into pieces, no lynching, or placing a tire around the neck like a flaming necklace. Her house wasn't torched.

The inspector dismissed the motive for Kwamboka's murder as wanting to rid Kabungu of a witch.

Fools, Dingiria thought. What cold-blooded fools. Because of Kwamboka's prominence, the police had to make a prompt arrest. These young men should have known that this time they wouldn't be protected by the police or the community. The police would have to produce results and they did.

****

INSPECTOR JAMES DINGIRIA READ another entry in Kwamboka's collection, this one about Anna and Richard, a story that he placed sometime in the 1970's.

The Okiamba home was far grander than the others he had so far visited in Kisii, a house with a living room, kitchen, dining room and several bedrooms, a modest home compared to that of the few "big men" in the area whose houses were two stories high with balconies on the second floor, but far beyond that of the typical homestead. This area was not as densely populated as other areas he had seen in Kisii, although by standards of his own region around Mt. Kilimanjaro, it was tightly packed, each farm not more than a couple of acres, the land given over to grazing of dairy cattle and planting maize, potatoes, millet, onions, fruit trees, groundnuts or tea.

He waited by the gate until Mrs. Okiamba quieted the barking dog and let him in. Once inside the house, Dingiria noticed a photo of Anna and her husband hanging high on the concrete wall. Other photos, of the couple and that of their son, were scattered through the living room that was filled with furniture bought from a shop outside Nairobi and fine, laced pillows. Cut flowers filled a vase. Anna, who was wearing a cardigan over a gray dress, told him that her husband wasn't at home at that moment.

"He is in Eldoret," Anna Okiamba said, "with our son. Our son lives there and has decided to return. This is the first time he has gone back since the violence. He was chased from that city because he was a Kisii and, thanks be to God, he is lucky to be alive."

Dingiria sat silently while Anna gathered enough strength to add quietly, "He almost went into the church that day. The Kenya Assembly of God, the place of the massacre. His fiancé wasn't so lucky. But he ran instead and found shelter in a friend's house."

"I hope all goes well for you and your family, Mrs. Okiamba," Dingiria said.

"I asked him to stay here, with us. We can build a house for him right here," she said, pointing towards the maize and cabbage garden. "Now I worry about two people and I am alone. I hope my husband persuades him to come home."

Dingiria brushed the leg of his pants with his hand.

"I've come to talk to you about Prof. Kwamboka," Dingiria said gently. "How did you know her?"

Anna explained that before the construction of the Malaika School, she bought dresses from a shop run by Rose Nyansarara.

"Also known as Malaika."

"Yes. That's what everyone called her. Angel."

"What can you tell me about Malaika?"

Malaika was young, good looking and vivacious.

"Everyone liked her," Anna said. Especially men, she thought with a twinge of jealousy.

Malaika met Kwamboka in a bus coming from Nakuru to Kisii after buying bolts of cloth for her shop. This was just when Kwamboka came home from America. She wanted to teach at the university but colleges were closed just then because of student strikes. Kwamboka hadn't been in Kisii for two decades and was interested in seeing what changes had been brought to the district.

"Kwamboka didn't have a family and had nowhere to stay."

"And Malaika's family?"

"Her father drowned in a boating accident. Her mother died in the psychiatric hospital in Nairobi."

So Malaika convinced Kwamboka to stay with her in the back of the shop. Kwamboka never left. Malaika thought Kwamboka should teach young Kisii children and not return to teaching in college. Although she was a college teacher, she always had an interest in young children. That's why her only published book was written for children.

"Who would want to move backwards?" Dingiria wondered, incredulous that a person with an advanced university degree would want to teach in a backwater primary school. It would be as if he returned to being a private and volunteered for duty in a dusty village in the northern frontier.

"The school was named after Malaika when she died," the inspector stated directly. "You said she was young."

"Yes."

"An accident?"

Anna was unsure how to answer. There was still a stigma attached to it.

"How did she die?" Dingiria insisted.

"The illness that takes away many young people."

Dingiria had little use for euphemisms. He was more accustomed to the straight talk of police work.

"AIDS," he said.

"This was new to us then. People were getting sick, and some people blamed Malaika for bringing the illness to the district."

****

LATER THAT DAY, WHEN Dingiria drove past the Malaika School, he saw a Mobile Voluntary Counselling and Testing truck stationed at  the playground. He stopped his Peugeot and asked the testers to tell him what they knew about the disease in the area. Purple VCT trucks were throughout Kenya and the staff provided on-the–spot testing for HIV/AIDS. They dispensed information about safe sex.

The counsellor told Dingiria that VCT had received a request from the school to set up on the playing field. They had been there for two weeks.

"Why would they want you here?" he asked.

The counsellor said that the school was concerned about the fate of the girls and wanted to protect their older girls from HIV/AIDS and other venereal diseases. VCT had a good reputation for reaching young people. While most welcomed the mobile van, not everyone wanted the testing and counselling services in Kabungu. Some didn't want to get tested—What good is it knowing that you are sentenced to death?—others didn't want to bring further attention to an area already blighted by a bad image. Some believed that only parents should talk about such matters and bringing knowledge about how the disease spread only encouraged promiscuity.

Dingiria asked the VCT counsellor what they had found. She shook her head. Warned that the figures weren't yet verified, she said that their testing showed that 17% of those between 15 and 35 tested positive, one of the highest incidents in the country.

****

"They know better now," Anna said. "Malaika didn't make anyone sick. She didn't bring it to Kisii."

"But they thought so at the time," the inspector said. Dingiria was familiar with Kisii's reputation of holding strong traditional beliefs, so he ventured, "And they thought she was a witch?"

"And Kwamboka, too. Two women not related and without a man in the same house. People can be ignorant and ugly sometimes. Jealousy can make people crazy."

Maybe he was too quick to rule out jealousy and witchcraft, after all, Dingiria thought. After a moment's reflection, he said to himself that he won't be dismissing this possibility. If that were the motive, there would be no reason to have concealed it from the murderers. Besides, the youths were paid too much to kill a witch.

****

*Richard Okiamba knew how to make money; he also knew how to spend it. In secondary school, while most students had little or no cash, Richard always had enough for sweets, for soda, for good afternoons in town. No one knew exactly where the money came from—some even suggested magendo but no one came out forthrightly to call him a thief.*

Richard's affable nature dispelled all jealousy and he was well thought of by students and teachers alike. Richard often bought small presents for his roommates, and he lavished gifts on every girlfriend. He brought them scarves, kangas, slippers or kiondos from Central Province. Once, he bought Yuneka a used but attractive cardigan. By the time he graduated from Birongo Secondary School, he had more girls interested in him than any boy, even those students who had fathers that visited on weekends in large European cars.

While those in Richard's location rode matatus or, worse, buses, he drove a small motorcycle to the market from his house. The underpowered vehicle puttered up hills, weighed down under Richard's well-trimmed body and a friend who invariably sat behind him. He kept the black 'pikipiki' for less than two years, then sold it to a former schoolmate and bought himself a larger, red Japanese model. He kept that for a short while, until he could buy his first car.

Richard's father died of pneumonia when he was twenty and, as the only son, he inherited the entire farm. He immediately sold a 'useless' piece of land to a desperate neighbour and re-invested the proceeds in another parcel of land discontinuous from his own, near Gesima. He leased that place to someone who paid him a part of the profits from the sale of milk, maize and vegetables. Richard now had enough money to marry Anna.

When he went to Kisii Town, he noticed a house that had been constructed near the Farmers' Training Centre, a house in which only a prosperous man could live: a concrete building containing as many rooms as children and protected from the pelting rain by a red tile roof. The gate at the roadside, which had lions wrought in iron, sheltered a profusion of flowers and fruit trees. This was Richard's dream house. As a result, he put only what little he needed into the maintenance of the house he owned and every other week went to Barclays' Bank to deposit money into a savings account.

Anna complained about the shabbiness of their house. Richard tried to convince his wife that saving was the most provident thing for them to do. That way, they would have the most glorious house in the district. Anna reluctantly agreed, insisting that at least they should have a comfortable bed instead of the old mattress they used. Richard laughed kindly and urged her to wait.

"Sometime soon," he said as he stroked her arm, "you will have the biggest bed you have ever seen."

"But I am sleeping now," she said.

This wasn't the marriage she had expected. The man who had wooed her was open with his wallet; money flew in all directions. This man, it seemed, was a person who made money only to make more money. All the beautiful things she had expected weren't forthcoming. Everything seemed to be for the future.

"We save now," he said, "so we will have more. This is how wealth is made, by investing wisely." She accepted his prudential ways begrudgingly. "I will buy a big piece of land and we will have a new house."

Over and over again he described his dream house—a patio, windows with glass, a couch and stuffed chairs, a table for the kitchen, another for the dining room and, he added with a great flourish, "A comfortable bed in every room." Each time Richard returned from Kisii Town, he embellished the details until the house seemed as real to Anna as it did to him.

Richard altered his plans the day he heard that the Kenya Tea Development Authority was planning to build a new factory not far from their house. Not only would it be cheaper to bring the leaves to the factory now and the road near their home be paved, but best of all, it would be possible to wire his house to the power line that would bring electricity to the factory.

"Do you know what this means, Anna?" he asked.

Anna didn't know. In truth, Richard didn't fully understand the implications either.

"We will have electricity in our house. Imagine! Electricity!"

Anna was taken aback by Richard's remark. She brought his coffee to the table and sat with him as they ate bread with margarine in the mid-afternoon.

"But we haven't even built the house yet," she said, "and you are already talking about electricity."

Richard blew over the top of the blue metal cup to cool his drink. He took a bite of bread and said, "The wire is going to be on the road right here. We don't have to wait for our house."

"You want electricity in this house?" Anna said. She got worried. "You spend no money on this house because you are saving for another. Now you want electricity. Why do you want electricity here when we are going to build another house soon?" Anna had assumed that she would be moving into the new house before their first baby arrived. But she had said nothing about this, not wanting to bring untoward attention to the fact that she still wasn't a mother.

"I went to town today and asked about plans for electricity in the area," he said. "It wasn't easy to find out. No one wants to talk. There are people who like keeping secrets. But with a little money I saw the maps and read what they are doing in Kisii."

He told her about the tea factory that was going to be built not far from their home. This meant that their house would now be closer to the electric power line than he had ever thought possible. They could easily hook-up and, with the money they had saved, be the first in their community to have electricity.

"But why do it here?" Anna expressed her annoyance. She brushed the breadcrumbs into her hand and tossed them out of the window. "Wouldn't it be better to build our other house and have the electricity there? We don't need it here when we are leaving so soon."

"I looked and looked on the maps and had my friend explain it to me," Richard said as he poured himself another cup of coffee from the pot. "Unfortunately, there won't be a wire run near our other shamba. There are no plans for a factory there. So the nearest wire will be miles away, no closer than it is now."

Anna hadn't thought about electricity before. She hadn't imagined a house without hurricane and pressure lanterns, rooms without candles and the need for a torch to find her way at night. Her dream house was having all rooms with running water, freshly painted walls and beautiful pictures.

"I am thinking," Richard continued, "that we can have electricity here and it would be as good as the new house we plan. I think electricity is better than a new house."

Anna said nothing. She didn't want to quarrel with her husband. It would be a matter of time to re-adjust to the new plan.

"I know we haven't done much to improve this house," Richard said. "But we can get running water and put in a choo. This can be a good house. More than a good house. It can be the best in the location."

Richard hadn't told Anna why he wanted electricity. He had wanted to be sure that it would really happen. Soon after the electric line was strung along the road not far from their house and Richard made arrangements to have his house connected, he told her. More than lighting up the house, Richard wanted a television set.

"You must watch television," he told Anna.

He needn't have encouraged her; she was eager enough to see for herself what she had only heard about. There was only one television in Kisii Town, at the Asian doctor's house. No one she knew had ever seen it but there were many conversations with friends about the machine. Richard didn't have to worry about convincing her of its virtues.

"We can learn so much from it," he said, oblivious to her eagerness to have a TV. "I visited a friend in Nakuru who has a television. He watches it every night. He has learned how they make cheese. There is news every night, from everywhere in the world. He has learned about fertilizer . . ."

Within a year, the house was connected to the power line. Anna bought a lamp for the living room and Richard drove his car to Nairobi to buy a television set. He shopped along Tom Mboya Street and River Road. At a shop along Muranga Road, near the roundabout, he found the one he wanted, a beautiful set and at the best price. He tied it down to the roof of the car and drove slowly back to Kisii, not stopping once.

They watched television every night. However, reception wasn't as good as it had been in Nakuru. No one had told him that the signal came from Nairobi and would have to beam across the Rift Valley and over the Mau Escarpment, arriving weakly and ghost-like on his set in Birongo. The picture faded in and out and sometimes Richard and Anna weren't sure what it was that they were watching.

They had the television no more than a week before the first visitor arrived. This was a neighbour from the far side of the hill who occasionally came to ask Richard's advice about one thing or another. Richard knew that his recent visit was only an excuse to view the box that sat on the table.

"So," the neighbour said. "You have a television."

"Anna," Richard said, "bring my friend here a bottle of Fanta. Come, sit down. At six o'clock there will be a telecast of the news."

"Are you sure you want to invite someone in to watch our television?" Anna asked later that night.

"They will be more jealous if we don't," he answered. "I say, we have something to share with our neighbours, we should do it."

Richard became more sought after than when he owned his pikipiki. Children loved him more than did the schoolgirls *who had received his teen-age largesse. In the shops, people inquired after his television set, as though it were a child of his. At the hotels, everyone asked him about the shows he was watching.*

*Richard and Anna began to receive guests, neighbours who had never visited before, relatives that they had thought were long dead, uncles and aunts they had never heard of, cousins whom they were sure had never been born. Anna couldn't buy enough Eliot's Bread to keep up with the demand and she began to stretch the coffee and tea a little further with each serving.*

*Richard enjoyed the attention his television brought. But when little Rachel arrived with her brothers, and twelve-year-old Alexander appeared with his six brothers and sisters, and every child whose two feet could carry him to their house began to arrive after breakfast and wait by the front step until the first broadcast of the day—then Richard began to have second thoughts. Their house more resembled a community centre than a domestic domicile, and Anna grumbled about all the work this caused her.*

*Richard pleaded with Anna to be more patient.*

*"But I do all the work," she said. "There's no one here to help me collect the water. And it is getting very expensive. Do you know how much it is costing?"*

*"We can't refuse, Anna," Richard said.*

*"I can't have people in the house all the time. If you want everyone to see your television, take it to the hotel."*

*Richard relented. At the bar he apologetically let everyone know that from now on the only ones allowed into his house would have to be invited: the custom of welcoming all guests, without invitation, had to give way to the exigencies of modern life. He explained that he wanted everyone to share in his good fortune, but it had become impossible for him and Anna to continue to open their door so widely. This didn't mean that they weren't welcome, he continued. All* they needed to do was make an appointment and he would schedule a time for them to watch television.

What seemed to Richard and Anna reasonable didn't seem sensible at all to the children who continued to congregate at their house every morning. Anna tried chasing them away from the door with gentle words. She told them not to stare through the windows. Each day the words became harsher, until one day she brandished a stick above her head and the children disappeared under the fence. But people who had only heard about the wonderful device or those who found the set more fascinating than the rules were compelling continued to come to their house. Richard tried explaining that this was a home, after all, not the Tuesday market.

Just as the television had brought them good will, the decision to limit who could watch with them brought down their neighbours' disapproval.

In a windstorm, the antennae was swept from their roof. Richard put it back up. When it was blown off a second time, they suspected a jealous neighbour. They were sure that night runners were behind the events when the harvest was thinner than expected. They consulted a diviner and employed a witch- smeller.

Richard built a fence around his property and, for the first time in the location, a lock was put on a door to a house. The closed fence didn't keep out the children; they crawled under the fence and waited, ever hopeful that they would get a glimpse of the flickering television.

Richard and Anna quarrelled as never before. Complaints against Richard were brought to the chief. Anna couldn't sell her produce at the local market. Their finances began to complain. Anna still didn't have a child.

Richard made a decision.

"We are going to have our dream house, after all, Anna," he said. Whatever money he now made he put aside to purchase a new place. Whatever money Anna made she saved. Within two years, Richard sold his farm and moved far from a main road, where land was cheaper but there was no electricity. Anna soon became pregnant and had a boy child.

They now live in a splendid home, a big house with red tiles and a flower garden. They have a wrought iron gate. At night-time, from the window of their living room, they can see houses on distant hills lit with electric bulbs. Regardless, , they are content to use candles and lanterns for light, rising early to milk the cows and pluck the tea leaves to bring to the roadside for collecting. Their television set has an honoured place in the living room. It rests on the mantle above the fireplace, sitting there blank and mute, never to be turned on again.

# The Way Water Flows

28 Feb. 2009

3 P.M

PASTOR ABUGA SHAKES the hands of the choir members as they take their seats under the white tent. Women who are on the lawn sit with their legs straight in front, many having taken off their shoes. A few have brought small wooden stools to sit upon. Men on the ground sit with their legs drawn up, their knees apart. Despite the heat, all the men who own suit jackets are wearing them and if they own ties, they are wearing these, too.

Dozens of umbrellas of red, yellow and blue panels, the kind that has become popular in recent years, are open. A few clouds drift in from the Lake Victoria basin, but it isn't enough to provide relief from the equatorial sun.

The Malaika School students, from baby class through to Standard Eight, who have gathered behind the church, leave and walk to the gate at the bottom of the slope. The two hundred girls form themselves into columns ten across and twenty deep. They are wearing checked blouses with wide, white collars and cotton skirts. Those who own shoes have shined them until they gleam. Music is heard and the girls march onto the field as guests make way for them the way water parts for a boat. At the head is Queenie Masanja playing an accordion. The girls are singing not solemnly but enthusiastically:

> There shall be showers of blessings
>
> Precious reviving again
>
> Over the hills and valleys
>
> Sound of abundance of rain
>
> Showers of blessing

Showers of blessing we need

Mercy drops round us are falling

But for the showers we plead

No one bothers to keep the baby class girls in order. They wander into the crowd only to have someone take their hands and bring them back to the marching formation.

When Nancy Nyaboke reports the story for the television news show, she says that more than 1,000 people are present for the professor's funeral. She had asked the police for an estimate of the crowd's size, but no one was authorized to give a count. Nyaboke's number goes uncontested and it becomes accepted as fact, the official figure of the day.

The coffin is festooned with flowers that were cut from the gardens around the Malaika School. A photograph of Kwamboka in front of the school with the first graduating class is placed amongst the flowers. Pastor Kennedy Okemwa, elegantly dressed and trim, holds the cordless microphone in his left hand and opens the program by welcoming everyone and thanking them for coming. He consults the notes he has placed on the wooden beam that runs across the front of the shelter and begins his introductory sermon. He speaks in Swahili, and then translates his comments into English. He addresses the guests in a conversational tone, more like a teacher than a preacher. Okemwa glances at his notes every few passages. He reaches down to keep the pages from flying off the beam in the breeze.

"If you were to have a chance to ask God a question, which one would you ask?"

Dingiria knows, but his faith doesn't take him that far. He relies upon solid techniques and verifiable facts, not faith. But maybe it is God, he thinks, who puts clues before him, so he can do his work. What would Okemwa or Abuga say about that? He never asked the priest in his own Anglican

Church in Taveta. What would these people who are God-infused tell him? That nothing is left to chance? Is that it? That everything happens for a purpose? His skepticism returns. If it is true, that God is responsible for everything, how can you explain the cruelty and corruption with which he is surrounded? He wants to bring justice to the world, that's why he is a policeman. But there would be no need for his profession if the world were just in the first place. If God were all good, there wouldn't be a need for his line of work. And how could these people of God explain the sports of nature—twins, albinos, and homosexuals? Dingiria has seen love and loyalty amongst all of society's outcasts. They have done nothing to deserve humiliation, ostracism or death.

The inspector quietly hums to himself the hymn now completed by the Sweet Chariot choir.

For a moment, Dingiria loses himself in reverie, indulging himself in nostalgia, something he seldom does, feeling what he did before he entered adulthood. The world as he now knows it is replaced, just fleetingly, by the smell of the cedar hedge and the distant call of mourning doves. He catches the sight of birds circling high in the lavender sky. He closes his eyes for an instant and sees violets laying down a purple carpet on the floor of the forests of the Taita Hills that he once knew so well; he recalls the song of the thrush from his childhood days. For the first time in years, he feels light, unburdened by the ugliness that his work pulls him into, the darkness that obscures the miracles that he now fleetingly experiences.

He hears Pastor Okemwa referring to Acts 24:15: " . . . and I have the same hope in God as these men, that there will be a resurrection of both the righteous and the wicked," and realizes how strongly he disagrees. The wicked should burn in hell forever, he says to himself. Better an avenging God than a forgiving one.

He worries when he says to himself, I know the devil exists, but I don't know about God.

Senior Inspector James Dingiria is drawn back to the reality before him: the funeral of a devoted teacher who has been murdered by thugs, by teenagers so desperate (or is it depraved?) that they care more about money than another's life.

He looks at the crowd and notes who is conversing with whom. He makes a mental note of who is present: the area chiefs, members of Parliament from all of the Kisii homeland, District Officers, a Provincial Officer, representatives from the departments of education, social services and health. The chief of police is there, his blue uniform covered with ribbons and medals.

Pastor Abuga, his bald head shining in the sun, walks over to the tent where the choir is seated. He tries to engage them in a conversation but no one pays attention to him. He walks to one of the smaller tents and fidgets with the buttons on his Nairobi-bought suit jacket.

Dingiria replays Okemwa's opening question. Which question should I have asked? Did I ask the right ones? Is there someone else I should have asked? Dingiria reviews the inquiries he conducted throughout the week leading up to today's service. He thinks back on his questioning Queenie Masanja at a lakeside snack shop in Kisumu two days ago.

\*\*\*\*

## 25 Feb. 2009

"YOUR NAME CAME UP in the course of the investigation," the inspector said to Queenie Masanja when he called to arrange a meeting with her. She suggested an ice cream shop far from the music school campus. She didn't want anyone who knew her to see her with a policeman.

The music teacher had registered no surprise. It was obvious to her that she would be implicated somehow. She was accustomed to being at the centre of controversy.

Masanja was the youngest of all those he questioned during the course of the investigation. She was more like a contemporary of his. And beautiful, he thought, with lustrous skin, a high forehead and warm eyes. Her hair hung around her shoulders in a hundred curls, at once both wild and managed, in a way he had never seen before but imagined had been inspired by a magazine photo. Dingiria couldn't remember enjoying the company of a woman in a long time.

His mind began to work in two directions. He had no wife and seldom did he meet anyone who attracted him. He proceeded lightly, holding himself back, just short of flirting.

There was no reason to hurry to get back to Kisii.

"I enjoy this, don't you?" he asked Masanja, who needed no coaxing in finishing her double scoop of vanilla ice cream. "I didn't see a shop in Kisii where you could get ice cream." This was the best he could do to make normal conversation.

Masanja told him that it was sold in the downtown supermarket.

He raised his eyebrows in thanks. What he meant was that he enjoyed being with her and he would want to get together with her in Kisii, after the investigation, to have dinner, but he couldn't say this to her, not now.

They said nothing more until she finished.

"Do you want more?" he asked

Yes, of course, she thought. She didn't often get to eat ice cream. But not with him, a policeman, even if was a polite, good looking and out of uniform.

Dingiria sensed a change between the two of them. He knew that he could never be anything but a policeman in her eyes. As casually as he was able, he moved on to his task and asked how she knew Prof. Kwamboka.

"I was a student of hers soon after she first started teaching in Kisii."

"You studied music at the school?" Dingiria couldn't remember when he had last asked a question out of personal, not professional interest.

"There were no music classes," Queenie said.

"I thought, perhaps, the professor brought some educational methods from America."

"She did. But not music. There was no money for instruments. I had the only one in the school."

"How did you get an instrument, if I may ask?"

She told him that she had uncle who worked in a pawnshop in Nairobi. An American left an accordion there when he returned home and Queenie's uncle brought it to her as a gift when he visited her mother in Kisii. She taught herself to play.

"I loved to lead the girls in marching around the school. I played the accordion and they followed." Masanja looked down at the table and changed her mind. She ordered another scoop of ice cream. "But you want to know about what happened at Sweet Chariot Resurrection Ministries."

Dingiria nodded. With Masanja's remark, he no longer looked at her as an attractive woman but simply as a useful witness in his investigation case.

"Pastor Abuga threatened Prof. Kwamboka with the wrath of God."

"Can you tell me what happened?"

It was because of her, she explained. Although she lives in Kisumu, she comes back to her parents' house in Kabungu as often as she can. When Finlay Abuga began his church, she, like many others, joined the joyous ministries. For Masanja, the emphasis upon contemporary gospel music was particularly interesting. Hymns at other churches were staid and lugubrious.

Abuga's good looks added to his appeal, as did his enthusiastic sermons. In addition to the call to piety and personal salvation, he stressed on the importance of providing for widows and orphans. Women abandoned by husbands and children left orphaned by AIDS were two pressing problems in the area and this call to duty fit well with Kisii customs.

"Religion that God our Father accepts as pure and faultless is this: to look after orphans and widows in their distress and to keep oneself from being polluted by the world. That's what Abuga preached."

This wasn't much different from the message of other preachers. Masanja went on to explain that what set Finlay Abuga apart were his sermons on financial prosperity as God's blessings. This resonated with the relatively prosperous households in the region of tea, pyrethrum and dairy cattle. "Those who open their hearts to Jesus and are born again," he preached, "will receive all the blessings of heaven and earth."

So the Sweet Chariot church filled with those who could afford elegant clothes, proving to all who could see that they were saved. And the pews were also filled with those who hoped that with enough fervour each Sunday they, too, would enjoy the world's bounty in good time.

All this—and the fact that Abuga seemed so successful— his clothes, his cars, his new, large house—was an advertisement for the truthfulness of his message in the eyes of many, Masanja said, and made Sweet Chariot the fastest growing church in the district. Abuga's church was presently acquiring more property to expand its present facility as it could just about accommodate all the worshippers who came each Sunday.

"This success led to animosity between Pastor Abuga and Pastor Okemwa," Dingiria stated as a hypothesis.

"I couldn't say."

"Won't say?" He wished he knew how to ask without challenging her. He held out hope of seeing her again on a different basis.

"Abuga was angry at Prof. Kwamboka because of me." Dingiria waited for her to continue. There was a long silence. "I didn't belong because of his message. Unlike others, I don't like him very much, but I loved the music."

"What happened that involved Prof. Kwamboka?" Dingiria insisted.

"He started to preach against homosexuals. He said that homosexuality isn't compatible with true Christianity. He stood in front of the congregation and called it a perversion of God's creation."

"Many say that," Dingiria said, remembering the spate of editorials that appeared in the national newspapers denouncing the ordination of gay priests in the Anglican Church. He knew that the new bill that consolidated sexual offenses, "carnal knowledge against the order of nature" carried a penalty of 5 to 14 years imprisonment.

"Yes, that's so," Masanja said. "But he went further. He made it more than a theological dispute. He said that those who accept such people are infecting Christianity and celebrating sin. Not only homosexuals, but anyone who doesn't condemn them as leading the world into the hands of the devil."

"Why did such sermons bother you?" Dingiria wasn't sure he wanted to know the full answer.

"This was dangerous. Abuga's sermons made homosexuality and witchcraft the same thing. He cited the Bible, saying 'Suffer not a witch to live.' He said that we should all do what it takes to protect ourselves and our families from the homosexual witch-devil spirits."

Dingiria allowed himself a personal expression. "I don't approve of homosexuals."

Masanja gave him a cutting look. "He was inciting people to lynching. Don't you see?"

He did and didn't like it, but his expression gave nothing away.

"Besides, this is supposed to be a Christian church," Masanja said indignantly.

"Just so," the inspector replied coolly, caught up in the discussion about homosexuality. "The Bible preaches against both homosexuals and witches." He didn't add that sex between men was also illegal under Section 162-165 of the penal code and some high politicians wanted to add lesbian relations to the statute. Dingiria didn't tell her that the president of Uganda had ordered the CID in his country to arrest homosexuals and there was a discussion about making homosexuality a capital offense.

"Christianity is joyous and forgiving," Masanja continued forcefully. "At least it should be. And it is in Pastor Okemwa's church. Let me tell you. The greatest sin is to ignore your neighbour. God's love is extended to everyone."

"So you disagreed with Pastor Abuga."

Masanja couldn't contain her laughter. "Yes, and I told him so. I said he was preaching hate, not love. That's when he expelled me from his church. Can you imagine that? He accused me of not being a good Christian and wouldn't let me sing with the choir or even attend services. Not that I want to ever set foot in that church again, not as long as he is there."

The inspector still didn't see what this had to do with Kwamboka.

"When the professor heard about what he had done, she went to the elders of the church and argued that I should be given a chance to defend myself. I told Prof. Kwamboka that

I didn't *want* to defend myself, but she said that there was a principle. If I was going to leave Sweet Chariot, she said to me, it should be because I reject them, not that Pastor Abuga throws me out. But she saw the pastor on her own. She said that his words would put Sungu Sungu against me. It was as much as saying that I was a homosexual myself and should be killed."

Dingiria, wrongly, thought that he was coming to Masanja's defense when he said, "The law is silent about sex between two women. Lesbian relations are not illegal." Dingiria wished he hadn't said that. He didn't want to be officious with her. His face flushed when he realized his error. "In any case, no one should take the law into their own hands," he said, as he fumbled for an apology. Then asked what happened when Prof. Kwamboka confronted him.

"He became righteous. He used the words of former President Moi who says that homosexuality is foreign and un-African. I wasn't there, but I heard that Abuga accused Prof. Kwamboka of bringing this evil to Kisii. He threatened her with biblical passages."

"How did Kwamboka react to this?"

"Well, before she could say anything, Abuga changed his mind. He wants to build his church, after all. He didn't want to alienate her. This wouldn't be good for his image. So he apologized and said that if she would join Sweet Chariots, he would rethink his sermons. The professor rejected his apologies and she didn't want to have anything to do with him after that. She wouldn't talk to him."

If Kwamboka had joined Okemwa's church after this incident, thereby threatening to undermine Sweet Chariot, then Abuga might have a motive to murder her. But Prof. Kwamboka wasn't a congregant in any church and she didn't denounce Abuga in public.

If anyone benefited from Kwamboka's death, it was Okemwa, who, as master of ceremonies at the funeral service, was bound to attract attention to his AICCD through his reputed association with her.

The detective asked Queenie Masanja about Kwamboka's interview regarding a story for her collection. Her name is attached to "The Way Water Flows."

"I told her about a cousin of mine, Leonard Gwaro. I didn't know she would use it."

"She did," Dingiria told Masanja. He wanted to end the conversation with an invitation to meet again. He said to her, "She called the story 'The Way the Water Flows" because of a curious thing. Did you know that water drains in one direction north of the equator and another to the south? And where are we now? I think the equator is just up the road. Am I right? Would you like to take a ride with me to see if this is true?"

Masanja didn't know what he was talking about and didn't trust his motives. She declined. Dingiria did drive the Peugeot ten miles north to the equator, following the directions given to him by Masanja. He thought that perhaps once he crossed into the northern hemisphere his mind would start spinning in the other direction and he would get more clarity about Prof. Kwamboka's murder. She told him to follow the Kakamega road to Vihiga, but Dingiria couldn't find the signboard indicating the geographical feature near the town. He asked at a local bar, but no one could agree where on the exact location of the equator. There once had been a marker, he was told, but it is long gone.

\*\*\*\*

AT THE POLICE STATION Inspector Dingiria went over the arrest portfolio. While he approved of swift justice, he found the speed at which the case against the three young men was progressing to be unsettling. There were confessions, to be sure. But there was no corroborating evidence, nothing to link them to the crime other than their word. No guns were found—or at least there was no record of any having been found. They could have be confiscated and re-sold by any one of the policemen who processed the men.

There was nothing in the file except the confessions, not even the arresting officers' notes.

The detective read their confessions again. They were identical, all three, word for word. While the statements may well be true, he concluded, they couldn't have been what they actually said. They were like templates that had been filled in, not spontaneous declarations of guilt. In addition, none of the papers had signatures.

Dingiria spent the night thinking about Kwamboka's case. But his dreams were about younger women.

****

*Kate looked at the large cardboard display in the window of the travel agency. It was a photograph of a giraffe and that of a bald black woman. Behind them, in a brilliant blue sky, floated a gaily-decorated hot air balloon. Kate had never thought of doing something so bold, but after watching the Academy Awards that March and going to the theatre to see Out of Africa, a safari now seemed as something within her reach, a vacation to this a land of breathtaking beauty and romance, and at that moment, outside the travel agency, Kate decided that she would celebrate her husband's serving her with divorce papers by buying a plane ticket to Kenya. The agent would recommend a group safari for her, and Kate would take the three-week package tour—airfare, hotel, meals and transfers included—at a price suitable for a schoolteacher. Kate had never been on a tour before. The agent said that the recommend tip for her safari guide was $10 a day.*

*It was summer in San Francisco, a time of fog and cold. School wouldn't open for another month and Kate dreaded the thought of September and needing to face her colleagues who only last month had thought of her, if not as a happily married woman, at least as a married woman. In June, at the last day of class, she left as Mrs. Gold and now she would return as what, she wondered, and as whom? She saw herself standing in front of the classroom greeting her new pupils. "Good morning, children," she would say as she wrote her name in large letters on the blackboard. "Last year you knew me as Mrs. Gold. I have a new name now. It is Ms. Tarnished."*

*If she had found just one friend to confide in, one colleague she could have unburdened herself to, then perhaps it could have been different. But Kate had always thought she valued her privacy and denied, even to herself, that something was wrong—with her marriage, with her husband.*

*As she examined the brochure, her spirits lifted like the wafting balloon across the African plains. Until the moment she had passed the travel agency as she walked down the street, Kate had had no thought of going anywhere, certainly not on safari. But there it was, as much a surprise as discovering her husband a philanderer. The longer she looked at the pamphlet, the more her senses sang with the possibilities. How good it would be to leave California, to visit the earth's last wild place, remote and quiet. Kate would spend three weeks in which, like a molting snake, she could shed the past. What others would know would be what she told them. She could live as an actor, in someone else's life. But this would be better than an actor's role for she could write her own script, too. She already began to see herself as, say, Meryl Streep sleeping under a mosquito net and slowly spinning fan, having several lovers and shooting lions. And when she returned home, she could continue to be the person she had chosen to become.*

*Kate took home a brochure. That night, as she sat at the table eating an omelette with French fries, she looked at the World Tours booklet. In it was another photo of a black woman wearing a beaded necklace. A proud Maasai, the booklet explained. She seemed so content to Kate, at peace,* at one with her place. But what did Kate know about this woman's life? She looked at the woman's shaved head, the many strands of orange, blue, yellow earrings that pulled her earlobes into large loops. Kate tried to imagine what it would be like to live the life of a Maasai woman. Did she worry about her husband leaving her for someone prettier, someone younger? Was she concerned about what her friends thought of her failure as a wife? Was this woman a good lover?

Did Africans know what love was?

Kate began to look for love from the moment she passed customs. The policewomen wore brimmed caps and other African women in the airport wore scarves. Nor did she see any bald women in the hotel lobby that night.

When Kate booked her trip in California, she had expressed concern to the travel agent about sharing a room with a stranger. The cost of a single supplement would have put the trip beyond her budget. There were two other single women on the trip. Each had requested a roommate. They weren't going to be alone in Africa, they said. So Kate wound up with a room of her own, and since all rooms were designed for two people, Kate always had a room for two, with a bed to spare.

Kate slept fitfully the first night. She had brief confused and disturbing dreams and was out of bed before the sky began to brighten. She showered, walked down the polished wooden steps from the third floor to the lobby and was sitting by a large window in the Thorn Tree dining room by 7 A.M. Here, at tables near her and on the street, she saw women more smartly dressed than she was, as her wrinkled cotton blouse and shorts were distinctly unfashionable in this city. She looked at their high heels, their clinging skirts, their Hermes-like scarves, and their beauty salon hairdos. She had been cutting her own hair for the last several years. She felt frumpy; her eyes swollen with fatigue.

*Kate watched the morning workers on their way to their glass office buildings as she stood on the sidewalk with her fellow travellers. She had been told to be out latest by eight, . She stood amidst a crowd near the newsstand at the hotel as tourists tried sorting their ways onto various safari vehicles. The street in front of the New Stanley was filled with cars and noisy diesel-engine buses. Kate coughed.*

*She recognized those on her trip from the ride from the airport, but she couldn,t remember their names. A van pulled up and the driver stepped out. He waved his hand above his head.*

*"World Tours! World Tours! This way. Good morning, ladies and gentlemen," he addressed them. "Here, madam, let me take that from you." He took a suitcase from an older woman and placed it beside a safari vehicle. "I am your guide and driver for the rest of the time that you will be here in Kenya. If you have any questions, please ask. I am here to make your safari a pleasant one. Thank you for being on time. So please listen to the instructions I'll give you." He had a broad smile and a way about him that made the travellers feel safe. "My name is Leonard. Leonard Gwaro."*

*Kate smiled to herself as the driver pronounced the first letter of his name as though it were an 'r.' She would continue to be bemused by the good-natured driver who now arranged the luggage in the back of the van as though they were pieces of a jigsaw puzzle. He removed each item several times until, at last, the entire luggage fit. Kate was embarrassed that her piece was larger than that of either couple. What was she thinking of, bringing half her wardrobe? She forgave herself, as she only had one week to prepare for the adventure. It had all happened so fast that she hardly believed that she was half the world away from California.*

*"OK, do I have all the luggage? All right, then. We are ready to begin our safari." Leonard said. He stood next to the van with the pictures of trumpeting elephants stencilled on the*

panel door, which he now opened. "I promise you that by dinner tonight you will have seen your first wild animal." He glanced at the three women. Kate stood alone.

Kate hadn't known what to expect from Africans, but whatever it was, it certainly wasn't a man wearing a pair of ironed jeans, pink polo shirt with an alligator logo and black leather sneakers with a Nike swoosh.

"There are bottles of soda and water for you in the cooler between the seats in the back." Leonard continued the lecture he delivered every three weeks to a new group of tourists. "There are enough seats in the van for all of you to sit comfortably. Those who sit by a window today change tomorrow so that others can also see. But don't worry. When we are in the game park I will pop open the top of the van and you will be able to stand up. So everyone will be comfortable. And everyone will see everything. Do you all know what the big five are?"

James, one of the other tourists, called out "elephant, rhino, lion, water buffalo and leopard."

"Right. And remember, it's Cape buffalo," Leonard gently corrected James. "Maybe we'll be lucky and see all of the five. Then your trip will be great."

Bob and Pam unfolded a map of Kenya and showed it to the driver/guide. "Show us where we're going," Bob commanded in the way that Americans sometimes do without malice.

Leonard pointed at the route to Amboseli, then retracing it back past Nairobi and on to Meru Park.

"Then we head west to Nakuru and finally Maasai Mara."

"Leonard," Leila said as soon as the driver paused. "I get motion sickness."

"My wife needs a front seat," James added, finishing his wife's thought the way Kate often wished her husband had.

Kate hadn't liked Leila since meeting her at the airport, the way she was dressed in safari clothes and sun hat, the

112

*ropey veins in her exposed legs. Kate sensed that Leonard was indulging her.*

"There is a passenger seat next to me," he said. "It's not the best seat for animal watching . . ."

"I also get car sick," Kate blurted falsely, surprising herself, but not wanting to concede anything to Leila. Kate moved from the newsstand to the side of the van, nearer to Leonard. "I can't sit in the back. I get very sick there."

Leila's husband walked from the sidewalk and stood next to Leonard, as the guide closed the hatch of the van.

"My wife must sit up front," he insisted. Kate disliked the whine in his voice. "When we signed up for this trip, I told the agent that my wife gets car sick and we were told that there would be no problem. They said my wife could get a seat in the front. We have been on many trips and there has never been a problem. There were cheaper tours we could have taken, you know."

Kate wondered about that. She decided to press her point.

"You," Kate said to Leila, "have your husband to hold your hand. If I don't get the seat next to Leonard, I think everyone in the van will have an unpleasant trip. I throw up easily. I don't think anyone paid to have vomit on their lap." Kate was thrilled with the daring character that emerged without design.

She put an abrupt stop to her end of the discussion by opening the door to the van on the passenger side while James continued to argue with Leonard. She climbed in, hoping that no one had seen the difficulty she had as she pulled herself into the high seat. She removed a well-used copy of a field guide to birds of East Africa she found on her seat. She placed it on the dashboard above the steering wheel.

"We will talk about this later," Leila's husband threatened Kate through the window. Kate looked straight ahead and *ignored his remark. While the others got into their places behind her, Kate combed her short blond hair and put sunglasses over her hazel eyes. She quickly glanced at herself in the side view mirror. She needed to shed several pounds, she thought.*

*"Tell me what your special interest is." Leonard turned slightly to Kate as he twisted the key in the ignition. "I will help make this a special safari." The van headed down the street, past the Hilton Hotel and the railroad yards out onto a two-lane highway. "Some want birds, some want flowers. On my last trip I had someone who only wanted to snap clouds. He never took a single snap of a lion."*

*"We'll see lions?"*

*"You never know about animals, but I will promise you that you will see a simba before you go home. And today you will see some animals, small ones."*

*Kate said little. The country was now open plains and the asphalt road in some disrepair. From the corner of her eye, she watched the driver hold the steering wheel with both hands as it shook beneath his grip. His hands were rough but his nails, while broken, were clean. She caught his eye momentarily as they both glanced into the rear-view mirror.*

*"Me myself," Leonard explained, "When I was at Utalii College, I liked birds. I made a special study of them."*

*"You went to college?" Kate thought he must have been lying.*

*"We have a college for people who work with tourists," he said. "It is difficult to get a place. Thousands apply each year, but only a few are chosen. But I'm such a good driver and mechanic that World Tours found a place for me."*

*"Oh," Kate remarked with a hint of amazement.*

*"I have been working for WT for twelve years."*

*"I saw the book you have on birds. I like birds, too," Kate added, thinking about the birds that flocked to her small*

lawn. She had never bothered to identify them and hoped that Leonard wouldnt ask her about them. She only knew the difference between a sparrow and a crow.

"If you want to look at the book to find a bird you see, be free. Or," he added, "ask me. I know all there is to know about birds."

The first request Kate made of Leonard wasnt about birds. It was at the Namanga market in Maasailand, at the turnoff to the game park in the shadow of Kilimanjaro. Kate wanted to know about the women there, those who sold the trinkets, why their heads were bald. Leonard laughed heartily.

«They just are,» he said. «The Maasai think its beautiful. Im not a Maasai myself.»

"Do you?" she asked. "Do you think a bald woman is beautiful?"

"I think all beautiful women are beautiful." He lightly touched Kates arm. "Do you see that bird?" Kate looked. She noted the contrast between his dark arm and her pale skin, the vendors shining pates, the orange and blue feathers of the bird. "It is called a superb starling." He laughed again. "I think all beautiful birds are beautiful."

The traders cajoled the tourists to enter their kiosks. "Look at this, madam," they called insistently. "Come, just look today. You dont have to buy. You are my first customer of the day. I have a special price for you." A young woman aggressively approached Kate with a handful of necklaces, the kind she had seen around the woman in the brochure, and thrust it in front of her. Kate withdrew. An elderly man reproached the woman. The woman walked away. «Do you want to buy?» Leonard asked Kate.

She thought of the necklace around her neck.

"Perhaps."

"I'll help you get the best price," Leonard offered.

"No, I dont think so," Kate said.

They walked a little further on the dirt path. "This cloth would look good on you," Leonard said, unfolding a kanga he removed from a rack displaying many cotton items.

"What does this mean?" Kate asked as she looked at the words across the bottom of the cloth.

Leonard looked at the purple and white cloth.

"It's difficult."

"What language is it?"

"Swahili," he said. "But I don't understand it all. 'Mpenzi Hana Kinyongo.' It is something about a person who loves but doesn't have something. I don't know."

"I could never wear it."

"You can use it as a tablecloth," Leonard replied. "That's what I do in my home."

Then Kate said, "That man. He treated the woman so rudely."

"She is his wife."

"He doesn't need to be so harsh." She didn't like her schoolteacher tone.

"If a man isn't harsh on his wife, he is looked down upon as a weakling," Leonard laughed.

Kate noted with only slight disapproval, "He's so much older than she is."

"Yes," Leonard said. "Several of these women here are his wives. Maybe she is his newest. He is a very rich man. He knows that many tourists complain when the women bother them. He is a good businessman. He knows the best way to catch bees is by honey."

Several wives? Kate wondered. She would ask later.

"There are many nice things to buy here," Leonard said to Kate. He led her into one of the shops. Kate hadn't thought of buying anything when she left California. She was shedding, not accumulating. As she walked around the shop, she saw

*Pam and Bob. They had purchased a five-foot tall wooden giraffe.*

*Leonard pointed out a tray of jewellery behind a glass case. "These are cheaper than in Nairobi," he explained.*

*"They are beautiful," she said.*

*"Let me show you, madam," the young man behind the counter said. "I'll make you a good price."*

*Leonard helped her with the gold clasp. Despite herself, Kate bought something for herself more costly than anything she had at home: a double strand tanzanite bracelet. The seller gave her a Maasai beaded bracelet as a gift for her wise choice.*

*They climbed back into the van. Kate removed her watch from her other wrist.*

*"That is a nice watch," Leonard commented as she dropped it into her fanny pack.*

*"It's not much," Kate said, immediately regretting the thoughtless response. She pulled the Swatch out and handed it to Leonard. "For your help with the shopping."*

*Leonard took the watch. "I'll keep it in here," he said, putting the watch in the glove compartment of the van. She felt worse. "Asante. Thank you, madam."*

*"Kate."*

*They left Namanga and drove down a road choking with white dust. The road undulated with gullies and dry riverbeds. Kate felt the grit between her teeth. Someone in the back began to cough.*

*"What is it?" Leila asked, as Leonard stopped the van.*

*"Why did we stop?" "Do you see something?" "Is something wrong?" "Is it a flat?"*

*"Over there," Leonard said to all the passengers. "Do you see the big tree in the distance? There is a tembo next to it. Elephant. Wait," he said as Pam and Bob took out their*

binoculars. Leonard turned off the engine. "I'll pop open the top." Those in the back were now able to stand. James removed his camera and screwed on a telephoto lens.

"Can you see?" Leonard asked Kate, who was on the far side from the animal. "Do you want my binoculars?" He gave them to her. She turned to her right and leaned across Leonard so as to look out his window. She could smell him and sense the warmth coming from him. She felt her shoulder pressed against the right side of his chest.

"Ready? Have you taken all your snaps?" he called behind. "I'll leave the top up now. Call when you want me to stop. I want you to go home with good photos."

The road was full of dips and curves. Clouds of powder-fine dust rose into the cab through the floorboards.

"It is good you sat in the front seat," Leonard said to Kate. "The ride is better. You are right. It is bumpy in the back. Here you won't get sick."

Kate gripped the door handle. She turned slightly, to look at her fellow travellers. Leila, who sat directly behind Leonard, had closed her eyes and rested against her husband. James caught Kate's eye and kissed his wife lightly on her head.

Leonard muttered something to himself in a language Kate didn't understand.

"Is there a problem?"

"Hakuna matata," he said. "No problem. Just a little thing." Leonard stopped the van, opened the door and walked to the back.

"What's wrong?" Leila asked.

Leonard asked the passengers to climb out.

"It's safe. Don't worry. The animals will stay far from you. Just don't walk away. I'll change the tire in no time."

Leonard unloaded the entire luggage to get to the spare. He attempted to loosen the lugs. Several tourist vans sped past *them, throwing small rocks and dust behind. The World Tour travellers found rest in the shade in a small grove of acacia trees by the roadside. Leonard distributed sodas that were in the vans cooler. Not until a driver of a Wildlife Trails van stopped to help did Leonard get the punctured tire off and the spare on.*

*Leonard apologized for the delay.*

*"I will try to get us everywhere on schedule," he said, "but 'kwa mapenzi ya mungu.' God will have His way." Leonard told them that they were now too late for lunch at the lodge. He would try to arrange something for them when they arrived. Another hour or so. A few grumbled, but most said they didn't mind. They had come for the adventure, after all, and here they were in the bush. This was why they came to Africa. They would have an exciting story to tell when they returned. Everyone but Kate took pictures of the van with Leonard resting his left hand on the blown tire.*

*Kate was hungry but said nothing. She would have another Coke.*

*They reached the Amboseli Park cement entrance and iron gate. Leonard got out of the van to pay the entrance fees. When he returned from the rangers' office, he asked everyone to alight.*

*"Another flat?" Pam asked.*

*Leonard explained that the trouble was with the vans motor and it was best that he tried to fix it before going on.*

*"I can repair it here but if it stops in the park, then it will be difficult."*

*The problem was that he wouldn't be able to get them to the lodge in several more hours.*

*"It is a short way to the lodge from here," he said.*

*"Do you want us to walk?" Judy with the white sunscreen on her face asked churlishly enough to make her displeasure known.*

"No one walks in the park," Leonard explained. "All the animals are wild. You don't want to be their lunch."

His sternness quieted objections. A look at the ranger on the roadside with his rifle on his shoulder dispelled the residual rumblings. "This isn't a zoo. You must stay in the van. It can be very dangerous."

The signboard next to the gate spelled out the rules for them. "We aren't going to miss a meal," Bob said.

"Hakuna matata. You are right," Leonard responded. "You'll be there in a short time. You're going to go in other vans."

By then, two other vans had pulled up at the entrance. Leonard talked to the other safari drivers. Bob and Pam went with an Italian group; James and Leila, Judy and Madge, the other single women, got a ride in an open-sided tour truck with young Germans.

"There's room for you with the two madams," Leonard said to Kate, indicating the last seat in the gallery.

"How long before you fix our van?" she asked, not moving.

"Kwa mapenzi ya mungu." Leonard laughed.

"Then sharmi a mango, for me, too," Kate said in faux Swahili. "I'll stay with you until it's done. You can't stay out here alone with the animals, can you?"

"In college I learned that the customer is always right."

Kate sat against a tree beside the ranger's station. She watched Leonard as he leaned over the engine.

Kate's back was beginning to ache from sitting so long. They were on their way from Amboseli, on the Tanzanian border, to a game park in the north of the country. It was an arduous ride. They by-passed Nairobi, made a short stop at the Blue Posts Hotel, in Thika, where the passengers ran to relieve themselves, then continued north through coffee fields, pineapple plantations and endless ridges of small farms.

*Where the country began to open to cattle ranches, Leonard said, as they crossed a speed bump (a sleeping policeman, as he called it), and said, "Here. We can stop." He pulled his van to the side of the road. "This is the equator. There is a toilet by the building over there. When you come back, if you want, give me your cameras. I'll snap you standing next to the sign. Put one foot on one side and the other foot on the other side. You are now standing in both hemispheres at the same time."*

*After the others had their pictures taken, Kate stood alone under the large yellow metal sign with a black silhouette of Africa.*

*Nyanyuki, Altitude 6,389 feet. 0° latitude.*

*Welcome to the Equator.*

*Leonard took her picture. Kate looked directly at the camera, her hands grabbing the pole and smiled.*

*"Here is something amazing," Leonard said to the group as a young man with a plastic bucket and a large funnel approached them. "He is a geology student."*

*"Good afternoon," the student introduced himself. "I'm Geoffrey Kamau."*

*Everyone was leery. They were tired of hawkers selling ebony carvings and copper bracelets. They had had enough of kangas, sheepskin rugs, and soapstone animals after Leonard had insisted they stop at the Namanga market on the way out of Amboseli and the curio shop next to the petrol station outside of Nairobi.*

*"I have a little show for you. You don't have to pay. There is no charge."*

*Geoffrey handed them a business card with his name on it and invited them to walk with him around the paved path. They stopped at a point parallel to the equator sign.*

*"How many of you know about the Coriolis effect?" he asked. No one answered. The student told them that if they*

121

*were lost in the woods they could know which hemisphere they were in if they knew about the Coriolis effect.*

*"Look at the vines. In the north, they grow clockwise around a tree,»"Geoffrey said. "In the south, they grow counter-clockwise. Now I will demonstrate to you in this very place the Coriolis effect. First, we will walk fifty meters north of the equator, then we will walk fifty meters south and finally we will come back to this very spot."*

*Intrigued, Kate followed along with the group. The student poured water into the funnel, then placed a small twig on top. The twig began to circle clockwise and drained into the bucket. He repeated the exercise on the other side of the equator. Now the twig turned counter-clockwise as it disappeared into the small whirlpool.*

*"Now we are standing directly on the equator," Geoffrey said as he placed the bucket directly on the equator line drawn on the sidewalk. He poured the water into the wide-mouth funnel. He carefully placed the light twig on the still water. The water began to drain. The twig stayed still, not circling, floating on the surface, as the water drained into the bucket. The twig floated to the edge of the whirlpool's vortex and plunged straight down.*

*Geoffrey had papers certifying that they had witnessed the Coriolis effect on the equator in Kenya. Everyone bought a certificate but Kate. She had forgotten her purse in the van.*

*AFTER SEEING AMBOSELI, MERU and Lake Nakuru, even thought they were now in Masai Mara, what had been touted as the highlight of the trip with its incredible herds of wildebeest, zebra and gazelles of various kinds, Kate no longer went on game drives. When the others left before dawn, she was still in bed. When they left for the evening game drive, she sat outdoors with a drink, looking on the land spread out before her, watching elephants come to the waterhole, gazelles keeping their distance. In the far distance was a clutch of giraffes. One morning she watched an orange and blue hot air balloon float over the savannah.*

*Kate preferred sitting in front of her tent alone and looking at the dun-coloured waist-high grass blow. Her travelling companions thought this lack of interest in animal viewings as peculiar. The trip wasn't inexpensive, after all. Why would someone come all this distance to stay alone without trying to see the wildlife as often as possible?*

*"Is everything all right, Kate?" Judy asked at lunch one day. "If you don't like being alone, we can rotate who stays with who," Madge added.*

*"Everything is fine, believe me."*

*Kate chose to eat in the dining room by herself. She had no desire for a conversation or explanation. Because she no longer went on viewing safaris, Leila now had the front seat twice a day, in the morning and evening game drives.*

*Kate found deep comfort in the silence of the days in the wild country, when all the lodge guests were driving around the park, and the warmth of human breath at night.*

*Madge and Judy were concerned about Kate and guessed that she must be heartsick and depressed. Kate had not revealed anything personal about her life in California. Because of this reticence, they concluded that she had been deeply hurt, perhaps a soured love, perhaps the death of someone close. Kate had become the prime topic of discussions at the dinner table, nudging out conversations about lions mating. Kate knew everyone was talking about her and she delighted in it. She would have been surprised to know that no one guessed as to the real cause of her distraction.*

*Leonard no longer slept in the drivers' quarters at the lodges. He went to her room in the lodge while all the guests were at the dining room. He was there for her when she returned after having taken her coffee and cheese on the veranda next to the fire. He stayed with her until two hours before sunrise. Leonard risked his job by being with her; Kate risked everything by confusing her vacation for her life.*

*At the end of the safari, Kate flew back to California only long enough to close out her accounts. Then she returned to Kenya to spend her life as Leonard's second wife, an idea she found intriguing since the day he explained polygamy to her and said that he had only one wife but one day he would have a second. She had no idea that she could experience a covetousness she never thought she possessed; she had no idea that as a non-citizen she wouldn't be able to get a work permit; and she never anticipated that she would be more lonely on the weeks  Leonard was away from home driving a van than she had ever been before and that she would beg him to spend more time with her.*

*Kate couldn't imagine that she would lose all her money in an ill-fated investment scheme in Leonard's matatu company or that Leonard would change the locks on their house one day when he came home and she was at the market. Kate became notorious in some Nairobi circles as the mad woman who stood mutely in front of the World Tours office for days, hoping to see her husband, waiting for him to return from safari. One day, she was no longer on the avenue in front of the safari company. World Tours—or perhaps Leonard— had called the police, who, seeing that she had no working permit, deported her back to California.*

# A Cloud of Butterflies

28 Feb. 2009

4 P.M

THE OPENING INVOCATION, prayers and welcome are finished. Pastor Kennedy Okemwa walks to the casket and extends his right hand towards heaven. "Amen," ripples through the crowd. Okemwa walks back to the dais, picks up a program and holds it in front of him. He uses the microphone in the stand and announces the speakers for the rest of the service. Inspector James Dingiria is scheduled to speak next to the last person. Okemwa welcomes the dignitaries who are present, a long list of personages and officials from the sub-location, locations, the entire Kisii district and the province. There are representatives from other schools— teachers, administrators and headmasters—owners of general stores, the supermarket and cyber café, the shoe shop, bookshop, the flour mill and tailor shop, a hotel owner, the coffin maker and clerics from several churches and the leader of Jamia Mosque, the large green and white structure near Daraja Mbili. Present is a manager from a furniture factory and the managers of tea factories and coffee cooperatives.

Okemwa says that if everything works correctly, there will be a telephone connection to Prof. Sarah Kwamboka's friend in America, which everyone will be able to hear. He announces that there is a guest book and encourages those who haven't yet signed to do so before leaving.

As Lucy Kombo speaks, Pastor Okemwa stands behind her, now consulting the program and making a note, looking at Lucy, his countenance at once sombre and re-assuring. Lucy talks about Kwamboka's dedication to Kisii, having given up an assured university position in America to teach young children in the area. She says that it must

125

have been part of God's plan because in New York she had met a friend, Lena Morrell, who has been raising money in the United States for the Malaika School for Little Angels. This money has provided scholarships so that no child is turned away for lack of fees. Each classroom has windows, there is a desk for each child, computers have been bought, a borehole dug so that the next drought won't cause hardships, treated mosquito nets have been given to all the pupils and their families, and the library is stocked with the latest books from Kenya's publishers.

"The manner in which she left us is exceedingly disturbing," Lucy concludes, as she puts back her sunglasses. "But we must hold on to what we know best. The greatest honour we can show her is to continue her work by re-dedicating ourselves to all the children—Kisii's and Kipsigis', wherever they are from, for our community and the nation of Kenya."

Okemwa says that they have Lena Morrell on the line. The connection to New York is working. Lena's voice is amplified over the black speakers. She says that Kwamboka left behind a great gift by raising the expectations of all girls. "What does a person get from the labour of her toil?" she asks and answered that it is found in the lives of all those who have graduated from the school. "She leaves behind a civilization."

Dingiria looks at his program. There are six more speakers scheduled. As he raises his head, he sees Finlay Abuga at the platform. He's not listed to speak. The young pastor has taken the portable microphone. Okemwa touches Abuga's shoulder and exchanges words with him. No one can hear what he says, but clearly the AICCD pastor is angry. Pastor Kennedy Okemwa rubs his goatee as the young pastor steps to the front of the sconce.

"I want to pay my respects to a woman who was an institution," Abuga says, ignoring Pastor Okemwa's protestations. "We are puzzled but never in despair. As we find in the scriptures, 'Praise be to the God and Father of our Lord Jesus Christ, the Father of compassion and the God of all comfort, who comforts us in all our troubles, so that we can comfort those in trouble with the comfort we ourselves have received from God.' Amen." He opens his eyes and looks at the audience. His resonant voice has begun to carry the crowd. Kisii's most popular preacher uses his good looks to his advantage and pours all his emotions into a sermon he has launched.

Okemwa, not knowing how long Abuga plans on preaching, looks at the program to make sure he isn't mistaken about Abuga being an interloper, steps off the stage and signals to the sound operator. The microphone in Abuga's hand no longer works. Abuga taps the cover of the microphone, looks at it and blows across the red cover. Okemwa returns to the platform and takes the microphone from Abuga who willingly gives the microphone to him. He thanks the senior pastor for allowing him to speak, "even though my name has been inadvertently omitted." Abuga is satisfied with his performance, believing that he succeeded in associating himself with Kwamboka and making Okemwa look petty by cutting him short. He thinks that if there were anyone who would be seen as being on the wrong side, it would now be Okemwa, for his lack of graciousness.

Two more speakers praise Kwamboka. The sky to the west beyond the church has darkened. The day has been long and Dingiria has only taken water in the more than six hours he has spent on the grounds. The inspector no longer pays full attention, more concerned about his announcement. His stomach begins to hurt.

Dr. Gladys Nyagaka, from the local health clinic, begins. She is wearing a long black skirt, a white jacket over a gray silk shirt, high heels and a pocketbook slung over her shoulder. Her sunglasses are lightly tinted, her hair is pulled up into a bun and around her wrists are tangles of copper bracelets. Her comments take an unexpected turn when she begins to relate a biblical parable. Dingiria listens.

"As a doctor I have seen much trouble. But we all know what trouble is," Nyagaka says. "Every one of us knows. In these times of increasing insecurity, we are all afraid. No house has been spared. I can see it on your faces." Dr. Nyagaka pauses for several seconds before continuing. "But in this passage from John 5, verse 4, the word 'troubled' means something different. This is water that is stirred by an angel's wings and it is healing water. It is written," she says, as she reads from a note she has taken from her shoulder bag, " 'For an angel went down at a certain season into the pool, and troubled the water; whosoever then first after the troubling of the water stepped in was made whole of whatsoever disease he had.' I have seen many traumas. There is too much in Kisii. So each one of us wants to wade into the troubled waters and be healed. One day, a man with many afflictions went down to the pool, but there was someone ahead of him. He went the next day and again there was someone before him. The afflicted man went many times, but he was always turned away. Finally, he complained and said, 'What am I to do? I need to be healed, but each time I go to the water there is someone ahead of me. My turn will never come and I will never be healed.' "

Thunder cracks and rumbles as the sky quickly turns from lavender to gray then black. Unlike the recent tease of clouds from the lake, now large raindrops fall.

Nyagaka hurries her remarks. "Jesus said to him, 'Pick up your bed and walk.' Pick up your bed and walk—that is the message. If we want to be healed, we have to do it ourselves. We can't wait for anyone else to help us."

What was she proposing? Dingiria asks himself. At first Dingiria mistakes her sermon as a message from Sweet Chariot Resurrection Ministries, but their emphasis is upon singing and material success, not healing. Whether this was her intent or not, the effect upon the inspector was immediate. He regained his courage and was no longer wavering. Reservations about what he was going to say drained away.

The inspector doesn't hear Dr. Nyagaka's conclusion, as there is a commotion in the crowd. The rain becomes steadier and thunder rolls across the hills. In the west, the sky flashes red and there is more thunder. There is good reason for concern. Kisii's red soil is ferrous and attracts lightning. Several years ago a dozen school children died on the playing field. The sky flashes and the sound equipment is unplugged. The men rush to pack it up and put it onto their truck. Motorists rush to their vehicles and those on the lawn find shelter in the church. Dingiria steps under the white tent. There is an animated discussion involving Lucy, the women who have spoken and Pastor Okemwa.

The girls are assembled and Queenie Masanja, playing her accordion, leads them down the slope to the road back to Kwamboka's house. A dozen people hurry to the coffin, lift it and, as quickly as they are able, bring it beside the house with the open grave. Dozens of people trail behind.

Inspector James Dingiria follows. He watches as the coffin is lowered into the waiting beside Malaika's grave. Pastor Okemwa, his hair dripping with rain, says a prayer. Soil is shovelled on the coffin until the grave is filled.

Dingiria has said nothing all day. He won't. He knows that by the end of the month he will have resigned his position.

****

The day before the funeral, Dingiria requested to talk to the prisoners again. He wanted to understand why the statements weren't in their own words. Who had prepared it for them? Why had they agreed? And, he wondered why they hadn't been mistreated like other prisoners, as often happened.

"They aren't here any longer," he was told by the officer in charge of the station.

This was unusual. Dingiria waited for further explanation.

"The case is closed. They've been released."

Dingiria couldn't find the right words to express his disgust. His eyes demanded an explanation from the office.

"We have their confessions," Dingiria said weakly.

The officer laughed. Nyang'wara stopped typing and looked up from his work.

"Sungu Sungu works under the community policing program. There is no way to bring crime under control without them."

"That program was abandoned by the government more than a year ago," Dingiria said.

"They are going to bring it back."

"But they haven't yet," Dingiria said, barely able to contain his anger. "As of today, Sungu Sungu are criminals, not activists. Those boys are murderers."

"Well," the officer said indifferently, "they're not here. They've been moved."

Dingiria walked to the window to get some fresh air. He knocked over a bunch of green bananas.

"Are they still in Kisii? I want to ask them some more questions. Where are they?"

The officer smiled through his tight lips and turned his palms upward. Was this a prayer, a supplication or a rude gesture?

"Who gave the order?"

"I can't tell you that," the officer said. "What I can say is that no one here objects to them being moved away."

So many palms had to be greased, Dingiria thought, that her murder couldn't have been a grudge, a matter of jealousy or the fear of witchcraft. Pastor Abuga didn't have such money nor would it have greatly benefited him. Lots of cash changed hands on the murder, the payment to the young men the least of it. Something substantial had to be gotten in return and Kwamboka had little.

The detective reviewed his notes and thought about the stories. But it was the professor's letter to her American friend that convinced Dingiria. He concluded that she wasn't the real target but was being used to send a message. The killing wasn't about Kwamboka at all. This would become clear shortly, Dingiria surmised, when the brick manufacturer representative would again offer to buy out the owner of the piece of property adjacent to the school. A Range Rover would arrive with two men, one with a smile on his face and shaking hands as he moves down the line of guests, and the other well-built and silent. There would be an expression of regret about the murder of the late professor—"What a pity she had to die"—and the factory would be built before the year was out.

Dingiria knew that to pursue the case any further was pointless. He will file his report, as aborted as it will be, and, he knew, it would disappear into the maw of a thousand unresolved cases. Dingiria thought about his future: a new assignment, to investigate another case, one that would amount to nothing if solving it no longer suited those in power. This violated his sense of everything he believed it meant to be a policeman.

Dingiria wished that Okemwa and Lucy had scheduled him earlier on the program. He wanted to tell everyone at the funeral that the thugs were no longer being held and they may be walking around Nairobi with some money in their pockets, although Dingiria believed it was more likely they would soon wind up like Kwamboka and there would be some story concocted about them resisting arrest after their escape. Revealing his conjectures (no, more than that; convictions, really) placed his own life in danger, but he had to cleanse himself. His police shield was no protection against death. He knew that when he joined the department. This year alone saw the death of more than 20 police officers, some at the hands of angry communities, some at the hands of fellow officers. He would be the object of the ire of Kwamboka's supporters; he would be seen as being responsible for the murderers' release. And many in the police force would find his comments a betrayal to their department. And those who made the payment would want him to disappear forever.

What Dingiria hadn't expected when he joined the police was how many there would be who didn't want him to do his job. Inspector James Dingiria had planned to use the service to say where his suspicions led him. That would be the last time he would wear his uniform until the day he would hand in his resignation, if he lived that long.

****

28 JANUARY 2009

*DEAR LENA,*

*I'M SO GLAD that we still write the old-fashioned way. While I'm always eager to get your e-mails and run to the school's computer each day to check to see what I've received from you, it is different when I hold in my hands the paper upon which you have written. It is almost like seeing you again when a letter appears and it is like touching you when I remove the paper from the envelope.*

*I seem to have run into a wall with my Kisii stories. I don't know who else to ask. I've importuned all those I know well and even some who are merely acquaintances. I'm beginning to feel a bit like a bore and I'm afraid people will run the other way when they see me approaching. But I just can't let go. I wish you were here, to tell me whether I am doing this for Kisii or for myself.*

*In a recent story I had to use a great deal of imagination. Queenie Masanja, you might remember, was the girl who played accordion at the school when you visited. She told me about a driver for a safari company and I thought I needed to present the life of a young Kisii man, since it is so typical for them to seek employment away from here. But I made up the American whole cloth. I'm a little afraid that it is a caricature. I'll attach it in my next e-mail to you. Let me know if you think I'm being unfair to the American woman. I don't want to malign the female sex. I'm still hoping that Queenie will find something to tell me. I'd like to know what it is like living as a single woman in a city like Kisumu.*

*I am now working on a story that I am calling 'A Cloud of Butterflies.' It is totally fictitious. You know that when I dreamed of a completed school there would be a garden full of hibiscus and bougainvillea, morning glories and bleeding hearts, rose bushes, cannas, tulip trees and jacaranda. That's all there now. And the lemon tree is grown and the scent of its flowers fills the air. But the sculpture that I had wanted, a winged bird carved out of gray stone, is still missing. Truth be told, I admire the stone carvers, but I think the committee agrees with me that we won't buy one until it is from a female artist. So unlike all the other stories I've collected, this one hasn't happened. Rather than being rooted in our history, it is a projection of our future. Of course, I will e-mail it to you once it is done.*

*My heart beats madly when I think of your visit. It's been too long since we've seen each other. I'm fixing up the house for you. Unfortunately, I've neglected it a little and this is a good excuse for me to take myself in hand and pay more attention to beautiful things.*

*The school is fine, as you know. I'm so proud of the governing committee. A couple of months ago, they were offered a large sum of money for the purchase of the playground from a company in Nairobi. The demand for bricks is great these days and they want to build a factory in Kabungu. You just won't believe what has happened to Kisii since you were here. It is more than bursting at its seams. It has exploded. But the committee was adamant. The girls are more important than money. I don't know what the school's neighbour is going to do about selling his farm.*

*So, see you soon, love.*

*Kwamboka*

\*\*\*\*

*Along with the other 100 hundred pupils from Standards Seven and Eight, Zipporah Ong'esa sat on the grass stretched in front of the school, her hands neatly folded on her lap. Her legs, like two limbs from an ebony tree, reflected the morning sun that now reached above the windbreak behind the several mud buildings. She could smell the aroma of carbolic soap on her freshly washed yellow blouse.*

*Zipporah had taken off the woollen cardigan she had worn earlier that morning when the air was still chilly. She placed it neatly beside her on the grass. By now the dew had burned away under the equatorial sun. Her skin glistened and turned damp with sweat.*

*The upper grade students were gathered on the grassy quadrangle in front of the school buildings to listen to the headmaster. The younger children continued their lessons as the older ones assembled. As soon as Mr. Motari walked from his office and crossed the yard to address the gathering, the chattering ceased. Only the birds ignored the headmaster.*

*"Good morning, children," Mr. Motari thundered, using his most formal intonation.*

*"Good morning, teacher," the pupils shouted in response, a single voice rolling down the hillside into the valley below.*

*"Today I have news to bring you," he began. He leaned heavily on his walking stick. "Visitors from all over the world come to Kenya." Motari spoke earnestly in his booming voice,*

134

loud enough to be heard by the men sawing soapstone at the quarry across the road. "Wageni from America, from Germany, from Japan, from Canada, from Italy. From everywhere; they come to Africa, to our nation, to our Kenya. And do you know why they come?"

"No, Mr. Motari," Zipporah responded in unison with all the students, having no idea as to what the headmaster was referring to. There was an Italian nun at the Catholic mission school nearby and not long ago there was a Peace Corps from Japan who lived in Tabaka. Every once in awhile, a European came to the co-operative store to buy carvings.

"They come to see our beautiful nation. They come to see the wonderful animals in our country," he bellowed. He rested on a wooden walking stick, a blonde cane with a lion carved into the handle. "Isn't that so, children?"

"Yes, Mr. Motari," they shouted.

"Yes, it is so," the headmaster continued.

A matatu overloaded with passengers could be heard struggling up the incline from Riosiri market.

"You are right. From all over they look at the lions, the giraffes, the monkeys. All the 'wanyama pori.' But our children, the children don't see what these visitors see. This isn't right, is it, children?" He now lifted the stick above his head, as though fending off one of the beasts of which he was speaking.

"No, Mr. Motari," all the children said again.

Zipporah fidgeted as she began to picture the visitors from abroad looking at animals, their pale skin, the green trees and grass. But she had no idea what Mr. Motari was getting at. They could see animals anytime they wanted. They weren't wealthy in Tabaka, but they weren't poor, either. Every family had at least one cow.

"You are more important than people who visit our country. Isn't that so?"

*More important? Zipporah thought. She had never considered the Kisii's important, certainly not herself or the students at her school, not people from Tabaka who were often looked down upon by others in Kisii as not being real Kisiis but an unacceptable mixture of Kisii and Luo customs and an odd accent. She wished she could wipe the sweat from her high forehead.*

*"Yes, Mr. Motari," the children said even more loudly than the first time.*

*The headmaster fingered his white beard, then adjusted his suit jacket and stood in front of the sweating, obedient children. He banged the walking stick on the red earth, as though angry at something Zipporah couldn't grasp. She began to think about animals and closed her eyes briefly. In her mind's eye, she saw the animals that her family and the neighbours kept on their farms—chickens, cows, goats and an occasional dog or cat.*

*Her mind began to drift as Mr. Motari continued. When she opened her eyes, she looked over the headmaster's shoulder and gazed at the green hills filled with coffee, millet and maize, passion fruits and bananas, beans and cabbage, eucalyptus, cypress, chestnut and gum trees. Just beyond the school's thorny hedge she knew there were men carving figures from stone carvings in her village, here in Tabaka. For years, Zipporah had watched them longingly as they carved rhinos, elephants and lions and she dreamed about what she could make from the beautiful stone. She, too, wanted to carve, like the men, but they would only let her wash and polish the stone when the carvings were done.*

*Headmaster Motari went on. "Would you rather look at a picture of a pineapple or eat a pineapple? A picture isn't the same as the real thing, everyone knows that. Then this is the same. Our children should taste what others are tasting, not look at pictures and think it is the same thing as eating. Isn't this right, children?"*

The sound of the hundred children's voices startled Zipporah. "Yes, Mr. Motari," they all said with gusto.

"No one should think they know what a pineapple tastes like until they bite it with their own teeth . Isn't this so, children?"

"Yes, Mr. Motari!"

"So you should see with your own eyes what the animals look like," he said. "The parents in Tabaka hold many harambees so we can pay our teachers' salaries. And even now we are planning to construct a new building with this money so everyone can study inside. No student will have to sit outside. But now we have been given a gift to pay for a safari. We can pay our teachers and build our building and we can go on a safari, too."

This caught her attention. Zipporah turned to listen. A safari? Zipporah had heard about money other schools had received from overseas. 'With those funds, they built latrines, repaired buildings or bought books for a library and chalk for the blackboard. A safari must be very important, indeed. She bent at her waist to better hear the headmaster.

"Pastor Nyanganyi," Motari continued. "He went to America last year. When he was there, he said that in Tabaka we don't have wild animals, only farms and stones for carvings. Pastor told them we have the best carvers in all of Africa, isn't this so?"

"Yes!"

"When he returned, he told me everyone in America thinks lions live by our doors and we have hyenas in our gardens. He said to the Americans, `No, there are no wild animals in Kisii.' Zipporah thought of elephants and giraffes. He brought them a few of the stone carvings as gifts. They said, "Yes, these are good carvings, indeed.' So now he has received a gift from the church he visited there. They want to help our children in Tabaka. They want to help our Kisii carvers."

*Zipporah didn't understand. "I met with the school committee and they have decided that the money is so that some of you can see the animals with your very own eyes, so you can know what you are carving, so you can taste for yourselves. We are going on safari to see 'wanyama pori."*

*Zipporah caught her breath and her eyes grew wide. She twisted her blue skirt between her fingers. Only now did she realize that the headmaster was talking about the children seeing wild animals with their own eyes. While she had seen pictures of Africa's animals in calendar photos and drawings of them in one of the books in her school library, all she could think was that they were like the cat at her farm but as large as a cow or perhaps like large rats. Now she was going to see for herself what lions, leopards, giraffes, rhinos gazelles, buffalos and wild pigs looked like.*

*The headmaster was right: there was no substitute for tasting the real thing.*

*Zipporah spoke excitedly to her friends about the safari.*

*"With our own eyes we will know," she said. But the others were indifferent. They weren't excited by the news although few expressed interest in going on the safari.*

*"No," her friend Pacifica said. "I don't want to go." Perhaps if the trip were to Nairobi to visit Parliament and meet the president and view glass skyscrapers with elevators that glide on the outside of the building or to Mombasa to look at ocean liners and battleships berthed at the port and see the Indian Ocean with colourful fish, there may have been some excitement. Pacifica would have been happy to go to Kisumu and go to the cinema. As it was, when they returned to the classroom, only Zipporah continued to talk about the headmaster's speech. She couldn't wait to see if the animals were anything at all like what she imagined them to be.*

*She went to Mr. Otieno to tell him of her desire.*

*"I'm sorry, Zipporah," her teacher told her. "You can't go. This trip isn't for you."*

*Zipporah could hardly believe what he had said. She wanted to ask him why she couldn't go, but when he put his head down to continue reading a book, she slowly walked out of the room. She thought about the rejection and reasoned that all the places were already filled. But when she heard that other teachers were still looking for students to go, she volunteered once again. She approached Otieno, full of great hope. He rejected her request again, without explanation.*

*"Go, Zipporah," he dismissed her. "I'm a busy man."*

*Zipporah stood by the hedge for a while. She saw a lorry being loaded with soapstone to be brought to Nairobi. She went to the headmaster's office.*

*She knocked on the open door.*

*"Hodi," she called, asking for permission to enter.*

*"You are?" Mr. Motari asked as he looked up to see who was standing in the doorway. He didn't know Zipporah, one of five hundred students at the school.*

*"Zipporah Ong'esa, sir," she replied. She stared at her bare feet. Not knowing what to do with her large, strong hands, Zipporah held them behind her back. "Standard Seven. Mr. Otieno is my teacher."*

*"Oh, yes," he said to her, putting down his pen and placing his hands on his desk. "What do you want, Zipporah? Did Mr. Otieno send you here?"*

*"No, sir," she said.*

*"Then what?" he asked her gently.*

*"I want to talk to you about the safari to see the animals."*

*"Oh, the field trip. Yes. I've arranged with the bus company just today when I was in Kisii Town this morning. We are going in two weeks," he explained to her what she already knew.*

*"Yes," she said, looking up from the floor. "That's what I want to speak to you about."*

"Well?"

"I want to go." Zipporah shifted on her foot. She surprised even herself with her comment. She, like most of the girls, was shy. Children didn't make requests like this of an elder. Students went to the headmaster only on errands, never with requests.

Mr. Motari looked at her quizzically. He wiped his forehead with a big handkerchief. Zipporah, too, began to sweat in the enclosed room.

"Mr. Otieno explained the purpose of the trip to your class, didn't he? "

"Yes, sir," she said.

«Then Im sure he said that this is to show the boys what animals look like so they can improve their carvings, so they can tell others how to make them better, so they can sell more, so we can bring wealth to our village.»

She hadnt heard this before: the trip was meant only for boys, although she should have guessed. Carving was not for girls; only boys and men were allowed to take the stone from the quarry to carve. Zipporah thought for a moment. She knew that customs change. She remembered her mother telling her that not long ago it was forbidden for a woman to eat eggs. Now she and her mother ate them every week.

«I also want to know what the animals look like, sir,» she said, undaunted by his objection, not revealing to him her secret. «All my life I wanted to see for myself what the animals look like, sir. Seeing a picture of a pineapple is not the same as eating a pineapple.»

Mr. Motari smiled. «This is very unusual, Zipporah.» He stood up behind his desk, leaned forward and said, «I have to think about it.»

«Please, sir,» she beseeched him.

Mr. Motari told her that he would talk to Mr. Otieno about her wish. But he didnt think it was possible for her to go.

*Zipporah thanked him and left his office.*

*That Saturday morning, after collecting firewood and water, Zipporah left her house and walked down the road to the Seventh Day Adventist church. She waited outside the church door until services were finished, then accosted Pastor Nyanganyi.*

*She introduced herself and said to the slightly built man with the receding hairline whose suit jacket was several sizes too large for him, «And all my life, I*ve looked at the carvings. Whenever I see a lion or an elephant, I look at them and ask myself what they must be like. I can*t imagine, but I want to know more than anything else . . .»*

*Pastor Nyanganyi placed his hand on her head, stopping her mid-sentence.*

*"I see that,» he said to her. «And why do you come to me?"*

*"Because I can*t go on the safari. The school won*t give me permission."*

*She told him what the headmaster had said to her. Nyanganyi stepped away from Zipporah, then looked at her thoughtfully.*

*"When I went to America and told them about Tabaka, people were surprised that we had never seen wild animals here," the pastor began, "I didn't ask them to send the gift, but when it arrived and I read the letter, nowhere in the letter does it say that Zipporah Ong'esa can't go on the safari. There isn't a word about Zipporah and there isn't a word about girls or boys. On Monday I will have a talk with your headmaster. I'll show him the letter. Maybe he can find where it says that Zipporah Ong'esa can't go on the safari. If he finds your name, then you will have to stay home. If he reads that in the letter, then you come to me." He let out a hearty laugh. Then he looked directly into her eyes and said,*

*"I know that he can find a place for you."* He placed his hand on top of her head again and offered a brief benediction.

*"Oh, thank you, thank you,"* she said. Zipporah ran home and told her mother that she was going on a bus trip from school to see the animals in the Maasai Mara .

*"That's good, Zippidy,"* her mother said with just a hint of excitement. She didn't want to bring bad luck with too much enthusiasm. «How many days will you be gone?" Her mother continued to ask other questions as they prepared dinner together. «Now wash these vegetables. The fire needs to be made."

*Zipporah happily did her work.*

*Pastor Nyanganyi, true to his word, came to the school on Monday. From the window of her classroom, she saw him come through the gate at the bottom of the hill and walk slowly to the school office. Zipporah didn't know what he said to the headmaster, but by the end of the week she had her place amongst those going on the trip.*

*A new white Toyota fifty-seat bus arrived about ten in the morning, newer than any of the commuter buses that normally travelled through the area. It parked on the grass patch strewn with soapstone in front of the cooperative store, by the'omotembe' tree, where only carvers were allowed to sit, a place reserved for men. The spare branches of the small tree were laced with red blossoms and offered scant shade to the men who sat there, a chisel in one hand, a block of stone in the other, a saw on the ground. There had never been a gathering such as this—children, parents, carvers, old women and men, nearly every curious person who lived near the crossroads. The gleaming vehicle was wondrous. Young children climbed the high step onto the bus and needed to be taken off, older children stood on their toes to peer into the windows, men looked silently at the elaborate instrument panel, and one put his hand through the driver's window to wiggle the gear shift.*

*Several people sat on the steps of the cinder block storage building. Other carvers continued to scrape the soft stone, their trousers, hair and feet covered with the dusty white chalk. Zipporah watched the men holding their works-in-progress placards, rubbing their fingers over the surfaces, smoothing the objects with sandpaper. She wondered if they wanted to go as much as she did.*

*Bundles containing the provisions for the trip were placed on the overhead racks. Mr. Motari discussed last minute details with Mr. Otieno, who would accompany the children to the game reserve, and then the headmaster addressed the pupils to remind them about their responsibilities.*

*"This is a great honour," he said. Most of all, he told them to look carefully so they could remember in their hands what they saw with their eyes.*

*"Taste so you can remember."*

*Zipporah glanced at her own hands. Yes, she would remember.*

*As soon as she sat down in the bus, she ran her palm across the maroon velour seats, the most fabulous material she had ever seen. She looked at the reflection of her face in the chrome bar on the seat in front of her. When the bus finally began down the dirt road towards the district border, Zipporah's heart beat so loudly she was sure others could hear the thumping. She tried to calm herself.*

*Not more than a half hour after departing, most of the pupils had fallen asleep in the stuffy vehicle. As they jounced along the dirt road, Zipporah's eyes were wide open, observing every change in the landscape. She noticed the shades of green of the landscape altering, as vegetable gardens became tea fields and shadows scudded across the tops of hills and across valley floors. She observed the small farms of Kisii open to wide wheat fields along the district border and then into an area of the forest where she couldn't find a single house in which a family lived.*

*The familiar-looking heart-shaped faces of her people were replaced with those of the high-cheek boned Maasai. The women she saw now were wearing more jewellery than Zipporah had ever seen in one place. There were orange, red, blue, yellow beads ringing the womens long necks and on their arms they wore coiled metal wire.*

*Making sure that no one could see her, Zipporah withdrew a handkerchief that she had placed in the pocket of her skirt, unfolded it carefully and took out a piece of soapstone she had hidden there. She rubbed the rock between her fingers. Zipporah couldn't wait until night when she would take out her secret knife from her bundle and quietly carve in the dark, again.*

*After passing the last village before beginning the descent down the rocky escarpment onto the savanna below, Zipporah could no longer keep her eyes open. She closed them now, hoping to nap briefly. When she opened them, they had already arrived at their campsite and some of the children were eating the bread and boiled eggs they had brought with them.*

*The first night, as they slept in the bus, through the windows of the vehicle, she heard the howling of hyenas and other sounds she had never heard before. Not until dawn broke did Zipporah learn from the driver that the bell-like sound, as though glass being delicately struck, was the mating calls of frogs.*

*After breakfast, they saw a herd of zebra, which reminded everyone of striped donkeys, gazelles of various sorts, some with flicking tails, others standing on hillocks looking into the distance as though they were guards. The students even saw a tiny pair of gazelles—dik-dik, they were told—that were no bigger than the dogs in Tabaka.*

*As they drove through the game reserve, they came across a herd of wildebeest more numerous than anyone could calculate. The bus stopped, the children got out and stood quietly as the thousands of bearded animals grazed on the dry grass. The children could hear nothing but bleats and grunts and snorts, as the cow-like animals chomped on the brown vegetation. Unexpectedly, the bus driver clapped his hands, startling both the children and the animals. The wildebeest bolted and galloped madly around the awe-struck children in a thunderous din, creating a dust cloud that rose, nearly turning the sky gray.*

*The sight of the first giraffe was beyond Zipporah's belief. She had never expected something so tall, so graceful in its run, the long head weaving with its gait, the beautiful patches, the long tongue stripping leaves from the top branches of thorny trees. Nor had she ever seen anything as powerful as the elephant uprooting the small fig tree, the crack of the snapping wood scaring Mr. Otieno and the driver, who quickly drove the bus down the path in reverse.*

*At the edge of the Mara River, they stood on the bluff above the water to watch hippos swimming in the eddy pools. The huge animals rose from the river and snorted, then disappeared from view again. A few exposed the upper parts of their bodies, their huge heads resting on the backs of underwater companions, the blubberous bodies tangled in a mass of pink and brown flesh. The children laughed as one hippo, which looked at them like an exceedingly ugly cow, walked to the riverbank on the far side.*

*Of all the things that Zipporah saw on the trip, the most amazing was what she first thought was a puff of white smoke whirling around a bush. As she approached the sweet smelling plant, she saw a cloud of butterflies dipping and swirling round and round in circles. Zipporah walked slowly, inching her way towards the butterflies, not wanting to frighten them away. Finally, she carefully placed her hands into the centre of the white swarm. To her delight, they fluttered around her arms, brushing softly against her dark skin with their powdered wings.*

*Many pupils were disappointed the next day, unhappy that they were on their way home and hadn't seen a lion or leopard. But Zipporah was more than satisfied. Her stone had already taken on the shape of a hippo, as she carved in the darkness that night, making an animal in elegant motion. She couldn't wait to find the right pieces of soapstone and begin her menagerie.*

*Leaving the Mara didn't matter; returning to Tabaka didn't matter. Where she lived, where she carved didn't matter. Whether anyone approved, whether she was scolded, whatever her friends might say about a girl carving—none of this made a difference to her. She was consumed and transformed by what she had seen and felt. The field trip had changed her forever.*

*Zipporah never really left the Mara, for she lived there in spirit, her hands burning, the animals buried deep inside her clambering to be released and made alive from the soft stone.*

*At first she carved at night, then in her house alone during the day and finally when her mother could see her. She couldn't stop herself from carving creatures made from soapstone. She and her mother kept this secret from the rest of the village, until there was no room in the house any longer. She gave a carving to Pacifica and shortly thereafter most of her friends owned a sculpture she had made.*

*One of her pieces, that of a running hippo, was taken to the co-operative store by her mother, and was bought by a tourist from Germany. It cost more money than any other carving of a similar size. He wanted others by the same carver, he said. He was a collector from Berlin.*

*From then on, Zipporah sold her carvings as quickly as she could make them, all of them made from rose-hued rock. However, those that she carved from the soft white rock, those of white butterflies, she kept for herself.*

# Other Titles by Arthur Dobrin

*Angles and Chambers* (poems), Cross-Cultural Communications, 1990

*Being Good and Doing Right* (ed.), University Press of America, 1993

*Business Ethics: The Right Way to Riches*, Hindi Granth Karyalay, 2009

*Convictions: Political Prisoners—Their Stories* (co-author), Orbis Books, 1981

*Ethical People and How They Get to Be That Way*, Cross-Cultural Communications, 1998

*Ethics for Everyone: How to Improve Your Moral I.Q.*, John Wiley & Sons, 2002

*Gentle Spears* (poems), Cross-Cultural Communications, 1980

*Getting Married the Way You Want* (co-author), Prentice-Hall, 1974

*Lace: Poetry from the Poor, the Homeless, the Aged, the Physically and  Emotionally Disabled* (ed.), Cross-Cultural Communications, 1979

*Love Is Stronger Than Death*, Columbia Publishing, 1986

*Love Your Neighbor: Stories of Values and Virtues*, Scholastic Books, 1999

*Malaika* (a novel), Jomo Kenyatta Foundation, 1998

*Religious Ethics* (ed.), Hindi Granth Karyalay, 2004

*Salted With Fire* (a novel), Oxford University Press, 1990

*Saying My Name Out Loud* (poems), Pleasure Dome Press, 1978

*Seeing Through Africa* (personal essays), Cross-Cultural Communications, 2004

*Spelling God With Two O's*: Inspirational Notes, Hindi Granth Karyalay, 2009

*Spiritual Timber* (aphorisms) (online publication), no publication date

*Sunbird* (poems), Cross-Cultural Communications, 1976

*Tea in a Blue Cup* (poems), Cross-Cultural Communications, 1999

*Teaching Right From Wrong; 40 Things You Can Do To Raise a Moral Child*, Berkley Books, 2001

*The God Within*, Ethica Press, 1977

*The Harder Right: Stories of Conscience and Choice*, Argo Navis, 2013

*The Lost Art of Happiness*, Prometheus Books, 2011

"The Role of Cooperatives in the Development of Rural Kenya" (monograph), in *Studies in Comparative International Development*, Rutgers University, 1970